CALUMET CITY P

P9-DEY-112

3 1613 00368 4233

How to Ruin a Summer Vacation

SIMONE ELKELES

How to Ruin a Summer Vacation

Woodbury, Minnesota

CALUMET CITY PUBLIC LIBRARY

How to Ruin a Summer Vacation © 2006 by Simone Elkeles. All rights reserved. No part of this book may be used or reproduced in any manner whatsoever, including Internet usage, without written permission from Flux except in the case of brief quotations embodied in critical articles and reviews.

First Edition
First Printing, 2006

Book design by Steffani Chambers
Cover design by Lisa Novak
Cover photograph © Ann Cutting/GettyImages.com
Editing by Rhiannon Ross

Flux, an imprint of Llewellyn Publications

Library of Congress Cataloging-in-Publication Data (pending)
ISBN-13: 978-0-7387-0961-1
ISBN-10: 0-7387-0961-1

This is a work of fiction. Names, characters, places, and incidents are either the product of the author's imagination or are used fictitiously, and any resemblance to actual persons, living or dead, business establishments, events, or locales is entirely coincidental

Flux
Llewellyn Publications
A Division of Llewellyn Worldwide, Ltd.
2143 Wooddale Drive, Dept. 0-7387-0961-1
Woodbury, MN 55125-2989, U.S.A.
www.fluxnow.com

Printed in the United States of America

In memory of my *aba* and hero,
Gidon Elkeles.
I miss you.

Acknowledgments

I want to thank Laurie DeMarino, Ruth Kaufman, Kathe Pate, and Patricia Rosemoor for suggesting I write this novel on our amazing writing retreat in Michigan. Other people I want to thank are Nadia Cornier, my wonderful agent who has become so much more, and Karen Harris and Marilyn Weigel, invaluable friends and writing pals along with the secret society Mag7 (if I told you who they all were I'd have to, you know . . .). Two people who have helped me more than I can ever repay, Amy Kahn and Randi Sak—I'm so lucky to have you ladies in my life and don't know what I've done to deserve the blessing of our friendship. Other friends and family I owe so much to: Liane Freed, Hadassah Alon, Michele Walters, Amy Gitles, Mary Friedman, Megan Atwood, Chicago-North RWA, for teaching me how to write, Nanci Martinez, for always being a supportive friend, and my editor, Andrew Karre.

A special thank you to Mely and Itamar Kandlik for welcoming me onto their moshav and opening up their home to me in Israel. You are incredible cousins and amazing people. This book could have never been written without your hospitality.

And finally to Samantha, Brett, Moshe, and Fran (aka Mom). Thank you for holding up my wings while I fly on this journey.

> *In a matter of seconds parents can change the course of your life.*

How does a relatively smart sixteen-year-old girl get stuck in a sucky situation she can't get out of? Well, as I sit at Chicago's O'Hare International Airport on a Monday afternoon during the one hour and forty-five minute delay, I think about the past twenty-four hours of my now messed-up life.

I was sitting in my room yesterday when my biological father, Ron, called. No, you don't get it . . . Ron *never* calls. Well, unless it's my birthday, and that was eight months ago.

You see, after their affair in college, my mom found out she was pregnant. She comes from money, and Ron . . . well, he doesn't. Mom, with her parents pushing her along, told Ron it would be best if he didn't have a big part in our lives. Boy, were they wrong. But the worst part is he gave up without even trying.

I know he puts money into an account for me. He also comes by to take me out to dinner for my birthdays. But so what? I want a father who'll always be there for me.

He used to come around more, but I finally told him to leave me alone so my mom could find me a real dad. I didn't really mean it; I guess I was just trying to test him. He failed miserably.

Well, the guy phones this time and tells my mom he wants to take me to Israel. *Israel!* You know, that little country in the Middle East that causes so much controversy. You don't have to TiVo the news to know Israel is a hotbed of international hostility.

I know I'm off on a tangent, so let's get back to what happened. My mom hands me the phone without so much as an "it's your dad" or "it's the guy who I had a one-night stand with, but never married" to warn me it was *him*.

I still remember what he said. "Hi, Amy. It's Ron."

"Who?" I answer.

I'm not trying to be a smartass, it just doesn't register that the guy who gave me fifty percent of my genes is actually calling me.

"Ron . . . Ron Barak," he says a bit louder and slower as if I'm a complete imbecile.

I freeze and end up saying nothing. Believe it or not, sometimes saying nothing actually works in my favor. I've learned this from years of practice. It makes people nervous and, well, better them than me. I huff loudly to let him know I'm still on the line.

"Amy?"

"Yeah?"

"Um, I just wanted you to know *dat* your *grandmudder* is sick," he says in his Israeli accent.

A faceless image of a small white-haired old lady who smells like baby powder and mildew, and whose life's goal is baking chocolate chip cookies, briefly races across my mind.

"I didn't know I had a grandmother," I say, emphasizing the 'th' because Ron, like every other Israeli I've ever met, can't say the 'th'—that sound is not in their language.

My mom's mom died shortly after I was born so I was one of those kids without a grandma. A pang of sorrow and self-pity from never knowing I had a grandma and now knowing she's 'sick' makes me feel yucky. But I shove those feelings into the back of my head where they're safe.

Ron clears his throat. "She lives in Israel and, uh, I'm going for the summer. I'd like to take you with me."

Israel?

"I'm not Jewish," I blurt out.

A little sound, like one of pain, escapes from his mouth before he says, "You don't have to be Jewish to go to Israel, Amy."

And you don't have to be a rocket scientist to know Israel is smack dab in the middle of a war zone. *A war zone!*

"Thanks for the offer, but I'm going to tennis camp this summer. Tell *Grandma* I hope she gets over her illness. Bye," I say and hang up.

Wouldn't you know it, not more than four seconds go by before the phone rings again. I know it's Ron. A little ironic he's hardly called twice in a year and here he is calling twice in a matter of seconds.

My mom picks up the phone in the living room. I try to listen through my bedroom door. I can't hear much. Just mumble, mumble, mumble. After about forty long minutes she comes knocking at my door and tells me to pack for Israel.

"You're kidding, right?"

"Amy, you can't avoid him forever. It's not fair."

Not fair? I cross my arms in front of my chest. "Excuse me, what's not fair is that you two didn't even *try* and live like parents. Don't talk to me about fairness."

I know I'm sixteen and should be over it by now, but I'm not. I never said I was perfect.

"Life isn't simple, you'll realize that when you're older," she says. "We've all made mistakes in the past, but it's time to mend them. You're going. It's already settled."

Panic starts to set in and I decide to take the guilt trip route.

"I'll be killed. Unless that's what you ultimately want—"

"Amy, stop the dramatics. He's promised me he'll keep you safe. It'll be a great experience."

I try for another two hours to get out of it, I really do. I should have known trying to argue with my mom would get me nothing except a sore throat.

I decide to call my best friend, Jessica. Supportive, understanding Jessica. "Hey, Amy, what's up?" a cheery voice answers on the other end of the line. Gotta love caller ID.

"My parents decided to ruin my life," I tell her.

"What do you mean 'parents'? Ron called?"

"Oh, yeah, he called. And somehow he convinced my mom to cancel my summer plans so he could take me to Israel. Could you just die?"

"Um, you don't really want to hear my opinion, Amy. Trust me."

My eyebrows furrow as I slowly realize Jessica, my very dearest friend in the world, isn't going to back me up one hundred and ten percent.

"It's a *war zone!*" I say it slowly so she gets the full impact.

Is that a laugh I hear on the other end of the line?

"Are you kidding?" Jessica says. "Heck, my mom goes to Tel Aviv every year to go shopping. She says they have the clearest diamonds ever cut. You know the little black dress I *love?* She got it for me there. They have the *best* European styles and—"

"I need support here, Jess, not some crap about diamonds and clothes," I say, cutting off her 'Israel is all that' speech. Jeez!

"Sorry. You're right," she says.

"Don't you ever watch the news?"

"Sure, Israel has its share of problems. But my parents say a lot of what we see on TV is propaganda. Just don't hang out at bus stops or go to coffee shops. Ron will keep you safe."

"Ha," I say.

"Are you mad at me?" Jess asks. "I could lie and tell you your life is ruined beyond repair. Would that make you feel better?"

Jessica is the only person who can make fun of me and get away with it. "You're just a laugh a minute, Jess. You know I'd never get mad at you, you're my BFF."

Although what does it say about our friendship when my BFF has no problems sending me into a war zone?

Less than twenty-four hours later I'm sitting in the airport waiting for our El Al Israel Airlines flight to start boarding.

Looking around, I watch a guy in a dark suit as he crouches on the floor and examines the underside of each row of benches. If he finds a bomb, will he know how to disarm it?

I glance at my biological father, the almost non-existent man in my life, who's reading the newspaper. He tried talking to me on the way to the airport. I cut him off by putting on my headphones and listening to my iPod.

As if he knows I'm staring at him, he puts his paper down and turns my way. His hair is short. It's thick and dark, just like mine. I know if he'd grow it out it would be curly, too. As hard as it is, I straighten my curly hair every morning. I hate my hair.

My mom's eyes are green, mine are blue. People say my eyes are such a bright blue they glow. I consider my eyes my best feature.

Unfortunately, the main thing I inherited from Mom is a big chest. Besides changing my hair, I'd like to have smaller boobs. When I play tennis, they get in the way. Have you ever tried a two-handed backhand with mongo boobs? They seriously should have handicaps in tennis for people with big chests.

When I get older maybe I'll get a reduction. But Jessica said during a boob reduction the doctor removes your whole areola . . . you know, that pinky part in the middle of your boob, and then after they take out the excess boob they reattach the areola.

I don't think I'd like my pinky parts detached at all.

As I think about detached areolas, I realize Ron is still looking at me. Although from the expression on his face he probably thinks I'm disgusted with *him*. I can't possibly explain I'm thinking of what I'd actually look like with detached pinky parts.

Anyway, I'm still mad at him for bringing me on this stupid trip in the first place. Because of him, I had to drop out of tennis camp this summer. Which means I probably won't make it on the high school team when tryouts start in the fall. I totally want to make the varsity team.

To make matters worse, Mitch, my boyfriend, won't even know I'm gone. He went camping with his dad for a couple weeks on a 'cell phone free' vacation. It's still a new relationship. If we're not together the rest of the summer, he just might find someone else who will be there for him.

I don't even know why Ron wants me to go with him. He doesn't even like me. Mom probably wanted me out of the house so she could have privacy with her latest guy.

Her current boyfriend, Marc with a 'c', thinks he's *the one*. *As if.* Doesn't he realize once Mom meets someone bigger or better he's out of the picture?

"I'm going to the bathroom," I say to Ron.

I really don't have to go, but I take my purse and walk down the hallway. When I get out of Ron's line of vision, I take out my trusty cell phone and keep walking. Mom got me the cell "for emergencies only."

I'm definitely feeling an emergency coming on.

2

*Being on an airplane for twelve
hours should be outlawed.*

I walk farther down the hallway and dial Jessica's number.

"Please be home," I pray as I stop by a window and look out at airplanes parked at their gates.

I usually don't pray; it's not in my nature. But desperate times call for desperate measures and I'm nothing if not flexible. Well, sometimes.

"Amy?"

I feel better already hearing her voice.

"Yeah, it's me. My flight is delayed."

"Are you still freaking out?"

"Yes. Tell me again why I shouldn't be worried?"

"Amy, it won't be so bad. If there was anything I could do . . ."

It's time to tell Jess of my plan. I just thought of it.

"There *is* one thing . . ."

"What is it?"

"Come get me at the airport. International terminal. I'll be hiding by the, uh, Air Iberia arrivals. Wait for me there."

"Then what?"

"Then I'll somehow get to go to tennis camp and . . . oh, I don't know. Ron wants me to be a perfect daughter, but he's the crappiest dad ever—"

My cell phone is being snatched out of my hand, cutting my 'crappy dad' speech short. The snatcher, of course, is none other than the crapper himself.

"Hey, give that back!" I say.

"Hello? Who is dis?" Ron barks into my phone like an army commander with a speech impediment.

I can't hear Jessica. I hope she doesn't answer him.

"Jessica, she'll call you when she can," he says, then snaps the cover shut.

He didn't even give me a chance to tell her to call Mitch so he knows I'm gone for the summer.

"Why? Why are you ruining my summer and taking me to Israel?"

He clips *my* phone to *his* back pocket.

"Because I want you to meet your *grandmudder* before it's too late. That's why."

So this has nothing to do with Ron wanting to get to know me and spend time with me. No *from now on I want to be the father I always should have been* from him.

I shouldn't be disappointed, but I am.

"Boarding now for El Al flight 001 to Tel Aviv with a connection in Newark," a voice with an Israeli accent blasts through the loudspeaker. "Passengers in rows *turdy*-five to forty-five please have your boarding cards and passports out for the attendants."

"Tell you what," Ron says. "I'll give you back the phone if you'll cooperate and get on that plane. Deal?"

As if I have any other option.

"Fine," I say and hold out my hand. At least I'll have my little connection to sanity and independence.

He hands me the phone and I reluctantly follow him on the plane.

Ron and I are assigned to row sixty, the last row. I'm kind of glad nobody will be sitting behind me so I can rest comfortably on the twelve-hour flight to Tel Aviv.

Unless, of course, a bomb is planted on the plane or terrorists hijack it and we die before we even get to the *war zone*. As I think about terrorists on the plane, I look over at Ron.

"I heard there are air marshals on all El Al flights," I say as I shove my backpack under the seat in front of me. "Is it true?"

I don't know if I've ever actually started a conversation with Ron before, and he seems stunned. He looks around to see if I'm asking someone else the question before he answers.

"El Al has always had air marshals."

"How many?" Because if there's only one air marshall against five terrorists, the air marshall is toast.

"A lot. Don't worry, El Al's security is second to none."

"Uh huh," I say, not very convinced as I look to my left at a guy with a mono-brow who looks pretty suspicious. Mr. Mono-brow smiles at me. His smile fades as I realize Ron is glaring at him.

After so many years with Ron as a 'birthday only' figure in my life, I feel like he doesn't have any right to say he's my dad. When I was younger and he came to take me for my annual birthday outing, I worshipped the ground he walked on. He was like this superhero who granted my every wish and treated me like a "princess for a day."

But by the time I realized a father should actually be there for you *every* day, I started resenting him. Last year I actually blew him off. I snuck out of the house, left a note I'd gone out with friends, and came back after dark.

My mom isn't easy. She throws men away for sport. But from what I know of Ron, he was once a commando in the Israeli Defense Forces.

A commando who's too chickenshit to fight for marriage to a woman he impregnated isn't worth much in my book.

I won't be like my mother when I'm older. I won't be like Ron, either.

Before long, we land in Newark to pick up more passengers. I've never eaten sardines, but when people start piling in and filling each and every empty spot on the plane, the disgusting little fishes come to mind. It boggles my mind how many people pack the plane to fly to a place on the warning list for American citizens.

When we lift off, I push that little button to recline my seat because I'm starting to get tired.

Only since we have the back row, I realize pretty quickly the back row *doesn't recline.* Okay, now this isn't funny. It's not just a short flight to Orlando. This is a whopping twelve-hour flight to a place I don't want to go to in the first place to meet a sick grandmother I didn't know existed in the first place. (That's two first places, I know, but at this point nothing in my life that bugs me is second place . . . it *all* takes first place.)

As I try and force the chair to recline for the fifth time and the person in front of me reclines theirs so far back I hardly have room for my legs, this feeling in the pit of my stomach makes me want to cry. I can't help it. I hate this plane, I hate Mom for making me come on this stupid trip, and I hate Ron for just about everything else.

After a few hours I get up to go to the bathroom, this time for real. Unfortunately, at least one hundred people have already used the facilities and the floor is full of little pieces of unflushed toilet paper shreds. To top it off (in the first place) the floor is full of these little droplets. Are the droplets pee or water? My Dansko clogs are not used to being subjected to this kind of abuse.

I go back to my seat and to my astonishment I'm finally able to get into a comfortable, albeit upright, sleeping position. Sleep right now would be bliss. The captain turns off all the lights and I close my eyes.

Someone yells, and I'm jerked awake from dreamland. Right above me, like practically in my face, is a Hasidic

Jew. You know, one of those guys who wears a black hat and coat and has long, curly sideburns running down his face and neck. Jessica (she's Jewish) told me they're ultra, ultra religious and try to follow all of God's six hundred or so rules. I have enough trouble following my mom's rules, let alone six hundred of God's.

It takes me a minute to realize his eyes are closed and he's praying. But he's not praying in his seat, he's praying right over mine. He's bobbing up and down, his eyes are shut, and his face is in total concentration. In fact, as my eyes focus in the dark, I realize all of the Hasidic Jews have congregated at the back of the plane to pray.

But it doesn't sound like prayers at all, more like some chant mixed with mumbling. They might not even be praying. But then one of the guys, I guess he's the leader, says a couple of words loudly and they all respond and keep on doing their mumbling chant. Yeah, they're praying.

Do they all have to do it at the same time?

And what are those straps on the back of their hands and arms or the box strapped to their forehead?

Now that I watch them more intently, I admire the men for being so devoted to their religion they would pray instead of sleep. Don't get me wrong, I admire it, but I wouldn't do it.

I look over at Ron, sound asleep. He's a good-looking man, if you like the dark, brooding kind of guy. Which I don't. My mother is pastey white and has blond hair and green eyes. She was probably in her "opposite" stage when she and my dad got together that fateful night.

I wonder if Ron wishes I wasn't born. If he'd chosen to stay at his cousin's dorm room at the University of Illinois, instead of following my mom to her sorority house seventeen years ago, then he wouldn't be stuck with a kid who resented him.

His eyes suddenly open and I sit back in my chair, pretending to watch the television screen in front of me without the headphones on my ears. I have one good thing to say about El Al Israel Airline—it has personal television screens embedded into the backs of every single seat. A miracle in its own right.

"I think you'll like it there," Ron says. "Even though I've lived in America for seventeen years, Israel will always be a part of me."

"And . . . ?" I say.

He shifts in his seat and looks at me straight on. "And your *grandmudder* will want it to be a part of you, too. Don't disappoint her."

I blink and give him my famous sneer, the one where my top lip curls up just the right amount. "You've got to be kidding. Don't disappoint *her*? I didn't know she existed before yesterday. What about her disappointing *me*? If you haven't forgotten, she hasn't been the doting grandma."

Believe me, I know people who have doting grandmas. Jessica's Grandma Pearl spent four years knitting her a blanket. *Four years*! And she's got arthritis. I wonder what Grandma Pearl would think if she knew Jessica lost her virginity to Michael Greenberg under the blanket she spent four years knitting with her crooked fingers.

Ron sighs and turns his attention to his little personal television screen. I note he's not wearing the headphones, either.

I sit back. There's a long silence, so long I think if I look at him I'll find him sleeping again.

"What do I call her?" I ask, still staring at the screen in front of me.

"She'll like it if you call her *Safta*. It means grandma in Hebrew."

"*Safta*," I say quietly to myself, trying out how the word sounds coming out of my mouth. Glancing over at the Sperm Donor, I notice he's nodding. His chin is raised and he's giving me a little smile like he's proud. Ugh!

Looking forward, I turn my personal TV to the channel showing how much longer until we land in Israel. Four hours and fifty-five minutes.

By this time the Hasidic Jews have gone back to their seats. I close my eyes again, thankfully drifting off to sleep.

Before I know it, the flight attendant says something in Hebrew. I wait until the information is repeated in English.

"We're starting our descent into Tel Aviv, please put your seats in the upright position . . ."

News flash—my seat has been in the upright position for the whole twelve-hour flight!

3

I'm not rude,
I'm just a teen with attitude.

The immigration officer inside Ben Gurion Airport in Tel Aviv asks Ron (who has dual Israeli and American citizenship) who I am.

"My daughter," he replies.

"Is she registered as an Israeli citizen?" she asks.

Is the woman joking? Me? An Israeli citizen? But when I see the serious look on the immigration officer's face, I panic. I've heard of Middle East countries where American kids are taken and aren't allowed to leave. I don't want to be Israeli. I want to go home, like right now!

I turn around, heading back to the plane. Hopefully the captain will let me back on . . . I'll go in the belly of the aircraft, in someone's luggage, in a damn animal carrier. Just get me out of here!

I'm almost at the door. Freedom is in sight when I feel a hand on my shoulder.

"Amy," Ron's familiar brooding voice says from behind me.

I turn around and face him. "They won't let me go back home, will they? You've kidnapped me to this country that wants me to be a citizen. Oh, God. They make everyone, even girls, go into the army at eighteen, right? I've heard that, don't try and deny it."

I know I'm sounding like a crazy sixteen-year-old right now, my voice several octaves higher than usual. I can't help it and I keep rambling.

"You're going to make me stay here and be drafted into the army, aren't you?"

I can just see them making me trade in my Abercrombie & Fitch for fatigues. My heart is beating fast and little droplets of sweat are running down my face. I swear they're not tears, just droplets of sweat.

"Ron, to be honest I doubt I'm even your kid. Did you ever get a paternity test? Because I saw a picture of this one guy my mom dated in college who looks just like me."

Ron looks at the ceiling and lets out a breath. When he looks back at me, his brown eyes are darker than usual. His jaw is clenched tight.

"Calm down, Amy. You're causing a scene."

"Dude," I say really tough, getting a grip on my voice. Now I sound like Angelina Jolie, in that movie where she kicks everyone's ass that crosses her. "I haven't even *started* to cause a scene."

A soldier with a very, very large machine gun walks up to us. He has an almost shaved head and I can tell just by looking at him he has a twitchy trigger finger. Great, my life is over, I'm going to be stuck in this third world country for the rest of my days . . . which are probably numbered now.

"*Mah carrah?*" the soldier says to Ron in Hebrew. It sounds either like "Macarena?" or "Kill Amy?" to me.

"*Ha'kol b'seder,*" Ron responds.

I never thought I'd be sorry I don't know Hebrew. In school, I take *Español.*

My heart is still racing when I ask, "What are you saying? What's going on?" I'm afraid of the answer, but I'm trying to be brave so I can tell the American Secret Service agents all the information I obtained before I escaped. The American government will want to know what's going on here, I'm sure of it.

"You're *not* an Israeli citizen," Ron says. "And you're not about to be drafted into any army."

"Then what did that soldier say to you?"

"He asked me what was wrong and I told him everything's fine. That was it."

Likely story, I think. But I follow him back to the immigration lady, mostly because he has a grip on my arm like a vise.

He speaks to the lady in Hebrew this time, probably to make sure I don't understand him. For all I know he's negotiating a deal to have me sold into child slavery. Although I consider myself pretty up-to-date on current events and I've never actually heard of Israeli child slavery.

Before long, the lady stamps my passport (which Mom had me get for emergency purposes a year ago and dummy me agreed to it, thinking she was secretly planning to take me to Jamaica or the Bahamas) and we head to the baggage claim area. We only have to walk twelve steps before we're there.

"Come with me while I get a cart," Ron orders.

"I'll just wait here," I say, because I want him to know I refuse to take parental orders from him.

He crosses his arms across his chest. "Amy, with the drama you just created back there I'm not about to play the trusting *fadder* right now."

I'm on a roll and can't resist. "You haven't been good at playing the loving *fadder,* either," I say, the words rolling off my tongue as if someone else is making me say them. "What kind of *fadder* can you play, Ron? You know, so I can recognize it when I see it."

Ron doesn't show anger too often, but even in the small amount of time I've spent with him I know by the sounds he makes or the change in his breathing patterns when something gets in his craw.

"Don't think you're too old to get punished by me, young lady."

I have my famous sneer ready. "Get a clue, Daddy Dearest. Being here with you is punishment enough."

I'm not usually this rude, truly I'm not. But my resentment toward Ron and insecurity about his fatherly love makes me act bitchy. I'm not even aware of it half the time. I guess if I'm rude to him, I'm giving him a reason not to love me.

Breathing pattern change. "Wait. Here. Or. Else," he says.

He stalks off, but I can't just stand here. I scan the airport and my eyes focus on the one thing most teenagers can't resist.

A Coke machine. (Insert harp music here, because that's what's playing inside my head.)

I walk through the crowd as if in a trance. Cold Cokes are calling out to me, "Amy, Amy, Amy. I know you're hot and cranky. Amy, Amy, Amy. I know you're sweating like a disgusting pig. Amy, Amy, Amy. I'll solve all of your problems."

I touch the Coke machine and immediately feel refreshed. I get ready to put my money in the inviting slot and for the first time in twenty-four hours I feel a smile coming on. It's comforting to know even in the Middle East Coke is available. Then I look at the price. My Coke addiction is about to cost me a sizeable amount of cash.

My mouth goes wide and I give a little shriek. "Seven dollars and eighty cents? That's robbery!"

"That's the price in shekels," a mother with two children hanging on her says in an Israeli accent. "Seven shekels and eighty ah-goo-roat."

"Shekels? Ah-goo-roat?" I don't have shekels. And I sure as hell don't have ah-goo-roats. Or goats if that's what she'd said.

I only have American dollars, but I find a sign that indicates a bank is in the airport. I follow the sign, heading straight for the bank. It's at the other end of the terminal. If I hurry, Ron won't even notice I'm gone.

But as I get to the bank, there's a line. To top it off, the biggest group of slowpokes are in front of me. I should go back to the baggage claim area, but I don't want to lose my spot in line. If these people would just move a little faster, I'd have my shekels and ah-goo-roats for my Coke in no time.

When I look at my watch, I wonder how many minutes I've been waiting. Ten? Twenty? It's so easy to lose track.

Finally, I'm next. I take a twenty-dollar bill out of my wallet and hand it to the banker dude.

"Passport?" he says.

"I just want to exchange money," I clarify.

"Yes, I understand. I need your passport number for the exchange."

"My . . . dad has it," I say. Ron took it after it was stamped so it wouldn't get lost. "Can't you just give me shekels without it?"

"No. Next," he says, then hands me my twenty back and looks behind me for the next customer.

My mouth drops open. I wasted all this time for a Coke and I still can't get one. Unbelievable.

I head back to the baggage claim and spot Ron. He's talking to two soldiers and when he looks my way, my first instinct is to run in the opposite direction. I did nothing wrong. Yes, he told me to stay put, but I swear I thought I'd only be gone a minute.

Call it teenage intuition, but somehow I don't think Ron will listen to my explanation with an open mind. He tells the soldiers something and then walks over to me, deliberately slow. I think he's taking so long because he's very likely thinking of ways to kill and dismember me. Do they teach Dismemberment 101 in commando school?

Ron finally reaches me and I brace myself. Sounds like "arrr" and "yuh" come out of his mouth, but then he turns toward the baggage claim carousel with our luggage taking a ride on it. I notice our bags are the only ones left. He yanks them off and tosses them on a cart as if they weigh two pounds.

My suitcase was over the weight limit. I know this because he had to pay over a hundred dollars extra to get it on the plane. Note to self: Ron is very strong.

I just watch him, waiting for his wrath to come. Believe me, I know it's coming. What's scary is I expected it to have come already.

A predictable parent is good. On the other hand, an unpredictable parent is a teenager's worst nightmare.

Now Ron storms off through the area marked "exit" pushing the cart with our bags.

And I'm still standing here, my feet planted on the ground in this strange airport.

Right about now it occurs to me my dear old daddy just one-upped me.

Damn.

Normally I'd wait it out as long as I could and make *him* sweat. Let him think I may not follow him *ever*. But as I glance at the two soldiers who are now walking toward me, I turn and hightail my ass right through the exit.

Goodbye pride, hello Israel.

4

*Change
makes me itch.*

I spot Ron by the car rental counter. He's not even concerned about me or looking to see if I followed him. I stand
next to him, but he doesn't acknowledge my presence.

I huff loudly.

He still doesn't look at me.

The lady at the counter hands him a key and tells him
something in Hebrew. He smiles at her, says "*Todah*," and
starts pushing the cart with our bags on it.

"I'm sorry," I say. "Now stop ignoring me."

He stops. "Does it ever occur to you that I worry about
you?"

I could lie, but what good would it do?

"Frankly, no," I say.

He runs his hand through his hair. Why do guys do that when they're frustrated? Do they think it's macho? I know why girls don't do it. They'd mess up their hair they spent half an hour trying to tame, that's why. And also girls don't have to pretend to be macho.

"Come on," he says. "By the time we reach the *moshav* it'll be dark."

"*Moshav?* What's a *moshav?*" Is it "shopping mall" in Hebrew? I mean, from what Jessica was telling me Israeli stores have the latest fashions from Europe. That black dress Jessica has *is* really awesome. I know I'd be selling out if I go with the Sperm Donor to a mall, but I keep thinking about all the great stuff I could bring back home.

It's funny, when I think about the mall, I forget about the terrorist bombing that could happen there.

As we drive along the highway in our red rented Subaru, it's also easy to forget this is a war zone. It looks like a highway in the middle of New Mexico or something like that.

As we hit the Tel Aviv area, traffic jam city starts. I look out the window at the tall buildings.

Ron points to the right. "That's the Azrieli Tower. It's the tallest building in the Middle East," he says proudly.

It might as well have a bull's-eye on it. "What a great terrorist target," I mumble, but then realize Ron is looking at me sideways. "Well, it is." I hope it's well protected, because 9/11 changed just about every American I know. I look out the window as we're passing high tech buildings with names of American companies on them.

"Israel doesn't look anything like a third world country," I say.

"She's not a third world country."

She? Israel is a "she"? Well, *she's* pretty darn modern. In fact, the traffic looks just like we have back home.

Although I realize pretty quickly Israelis need to go to road rage school.

They're all yelling at each other out the windows and giving each other the finger when cut off. And I shriek when a bunch of people on those little motor scooters and motorcycles ride right in between the cars. They're not even weaving in the lanes; they're riding on the lines themselves!

"We've been in the car an hour. When are we gonna get there?" I say.

"In another hour or so."

"You never answered me. What's a *moshav?* Is it a mall?"

He laughs and I don't think a *moshav* is a mall anymore.

"Have you ever heard of a *kibbutz?*" he asks me.

"You mean community living where people share *everything?* Listen, if you're taking me to a sick commune—"

"Why do you always do that?"

"Do what?"

"Overreact."

"For your information, I do *not* overreact. Mom overreacts, especially when it comes to me coming home after my curfew. Oh, yeah, you wouldn't know anything about that because you're never there," I say sarcastically.

Silence.

"Then why don't you come live with me for a while," he challenges.

Me, live with him? "Do you have a girlfriend?" I ask. I want him to say no because I have plans for him and Mom. It'll be easier if he's not attached.

"No. Do you have a boyfriend?"

Now wait one second. When did it turn around to him asking me the questions? "Maybe."

"Amy, when are you going to learn to trust me? I'm not the enemy, you know."

"Then tell me what a *moshav* is."

"A *moshav* is a close-knit community. It's similar to a kibbutz, but everyone owns their own property and farmland. The money isn't shared or pooled together."

Still sounds like a commune to me.

"I hope we're not staying there for long," I say. "I need to take a shower at the hotel and unpack. I have stuff probably melting in this heat—"

"We're not staying at a hotel," he says.

Now I'm going to overreact.

"What?" I say really loudly.

"We'll be staying with your aunt, uncle, cousins, and *Safta*." He pauses. I know what's coming next, I do. But I'm not mentally prepared for it when he adds, "At the *moshav*."

"Let's set the record straight, Ron. I'm an all-American girl with red, white, and blue blood running through these veins. I do not stay at places called *moshavs*. Unless I've signed up for the Girl Scouts, which I didn't. I need amenities. Amenities! Do you know what those are?"

"Yes. But don't expect many where we're going. Last time I visited, only one family on the *moshav* had electricity and it wasn't mine."

I open the glove compartment.

"What are you doing?" Ron asks.

"Looking for a map so I know which direction to go when I escape from the *moshav*," I say.

He chuckles.

"Ha, ha, funny, funny. I bet you won't be laughing when you wake up one morning and find I've gone back to civilization."

Ron pats my knee with his hand. "I was just kidding, Amy. They have electricity."

Kidding? Ron was *kidding* with me?

"I knew you were joking. Do you actually think I'm that gullible?"

He doesn't answer, but I know he knows the truth by the quirky way his mouth is moving.

"Will you at least give me the keys to your car so I can drive myself to a mall?"

"Sorry. Driving age here is eighteen."

"What!"

"I'll take you wherever you want to go. Don't worry. Besides, if you get lost you won't know how to get back."

Good, I think to myself. Getting lost sounds like a great idea.

I sigh and look out the window. On one side of the car is the Mediterranean Sea and on the other side are mountains with houses built into them. If I was in a better mood

I might even think the scenery is beautiful, but I'm cranky and tired and my butt is numb.

I start doing my butt exercises. I was watching a late night talk show a couple of years ago when some action star, maybe Steven Seagal or Antonio Banderas, was talking about how they do butt exercises while in the car.

Just tighten, then release. Tighten. Release. Tighten. Release. I'm "feeling it burn," but after ten minutes my butt cheeks start to quiver on the tighten part and I stop.

By now we've taken a turn away from the sea and all around us are small trees in rows.

"What are those?" I ask.

"Olive trees."

"I hate olives."

"I love them."

Figures. "I hope you're not one of those pit-spitters."

"Huh?"

"You know, those people who spit out the pit right in front of other people at the table. That's totally gross."

He doesn't answer. I would bet my grandmother's underpants Ron is a pit-spitter.

"What kind of food do you like?" he asks. "I'm sure I can get it for you."

"Sushi."

"You mean raw fish?" he asks, wincing.

"Yep."

I used to hate it. When Mom first had me try it I gagged and spit it out (into my napkin, very discreetly I might add, unlike gross pit-spitters). Mom loves sushi. I guess it's like alcohol. You want to puke the first time you have it, but then it grows on you and you like it. It's probably why they say there's a thin line between love and hate. Now I don't just like sushi, I crave it. Ron obviously needs to be introduced to sushi with a professional sushi-eater like me.

We're now driving through the mountains on an extremely curvy road and I'm getting nauseous. The last time I noticed civilization was about fifteen minutes ago.

We wind our way down one mountain and stop at the road leading to another one. I read a sign with the words MOSHAV MENORA in English and some words in Hebrew on it.

Ron takes the road to Moshav Menora. Now the place looks like Switzerland, with grassy hills surrounding us on all sides.

He stops at a scenic rest stop built into the mountain.

"This is it?" I ask.

He turns to me and takes the key out of the ignition. "This is the Golan Heights, a very special and beautiful place. Let's go see the view."

"Do I have to?" I ask. "I got to pee."

"Can you hold it for a few minutes longer? I really need to talk with you before you meet my family."

This I have to hear. I open the car door and walk outside. We stroll in silence to the edge of the mountain. When I look over the edge, it reminds me of a scene from a postcard.

"They don't know about you," Ron blurts out.

Huh?

"Who doesn't know about me?"

"My *mudder*, my *brudder* and his wife . . ."

A pang of pain stabs my chest as if something pierced it. My heart starts beating fast and I'm breathing heavily. "Why?" I whisper, barely able to get the words out.

"It's complicated," he says, and then looks away from me. "You see, when I came to America I wanted to prove to everyone back here I could make it. You know, The American Dream."

"And you didn't expect me to come along and ruin your dream," I say.

"I met your mom the first weekend I was in the U.S. I was a cocky Israeli who just wanted to have a good time. A few months later I found out I was going to be a *fadder*."

I start walking away from him. What does he want me to do, apologize for being born?

"I hate you," I say as I head back to the car. I wipe the stupid tears I can't help from falling down my cheeks.

"Amy, please. For once let me set the record straight—"

"Just unlock the door." I hear the click and get inside the car. He's looking at me like he wants to explain more, but I don't want to hear it. "Let's go already!" I yell.

He gets back in the car and we ride up to the top of the mountain. I thought I was ready to meet Ron's family, but now all I want to do is crawl into a hole.

Because he's not just going to introduce me to his family, he's going to tell them for the first time he has an illegitimate daughter.

5

If I close my eyes, will life stop
spinning out of control?

We reach a gate and a guy with a large machine gun comes up to our car. I've never even seen a machine gun before today and cringe every time I think about what they're used for.

Ron says something in Hebrew. The guy smiles and signals for the gate to open. We drive down a dirt road on top of the mountain and pass six rows of houses. There are about seven to ten houses down each road on either side. Ron turns down one of them and parks in front of a house.

"I'm not going in until you tell them who I am," I say.

I think he's going to argue and I ready myself for a fight. But Ron just says, "Fair enough."

He gets out of the car and I stay put. I watch as he enters the small one-story house.

The windows are open in the car, but there's no breeze. And it's not only hot, I think the devil himself must live on this mountain because sweat is pouring down my face, neck, and chest. My Abercrombie & Fitch shirt has wet marks on it already from disgusting armpit sweat.

How can these people stand the heat? I look at my nail before biting on it. What is Ron saying to them? Is he sweating as much as I am? I hope so.

I step out of the car and lean against the side of it, listening for the scolding *Safta* should be giving Ron. Boy is he going to get it. If I were *Safta* I'd rip him a new one for denying her, well, me. But I don't hear yelling. In fact, I don't hear much coming from the house.

Instead, something hits my arm. Hard.

"Hey!" I yell and panic.

I'm not stupid, I know it's not a bullet. Not that I wouldn't be surprised if Ron's family decided "do away" with his illegitimate daughter once they heard the truth.

As I have that thought, I look down and see the offending object.

A soccer ball.

"*Tizreki le'kan*," a voice bellows from behind the car. As if I can understand. But I can't, so I ignore it. Besides, I already feel a bruise forming on my arm.

The sound of running footsteps echoes before I'm face to face with an Israeli boy about my age.

"*Shalom*," he says.

He's wearing jeans, has a dusty and ripped white T-shirt on, and is wearing Greek sandals. You know, the ones like the Greek philosophers wore. But that's not the worst part. The guy is wearing white socks along with the sandals. Socks with sandals! Seeing that makes me laugh so I look up at his face instead of his feet. I don't want to insult the guy.

"Hi," I say.

Does he speak English? I don't know so I just stand there in silence.

Two more boys run up to us. One starts to talk to the boy in Hebrew but becomes silent when he notices me.

"I America," I say slowly and loud like I'm talking to a chimpanzee. I'm hoping by some miracle they'll understand me.

They turn to each other with confused looks on their faces and I realize these next three months are going to be like living in a bubble. A bubble with people who don't understand a word I'm saying, except for the Sperm Donor. Could my summer vacation be ruined more?

The first boy steps closer to me. He has dark blond hair and a rugged, boyish grin. I know, I know, rugged and boyish don't really go together. But on this guy it does, trust me. "You speak English?" he asks with a heavy accent.

Huh? "Yes. Do you?"

"Yes. But what does 'I America' mean?"

"Nothing. Just forget it."

"You a friend us not?" he asks.

Huh? Obviously his English isn't good. Was he asking if I'm a friend or not? I'm almost afraid to say no. "Yes."

The second guy turns to me. "What's your name?"

"Amy."

"Hi Amy, I'm Doo-Doo," he says. Then he points to the other two guys. "And this is Moron and O'dead."

Now, I've never said these four words in a row before. In fact, I don't think they've ever come out of someone less than the age of sixty, but they come out of my mouth almost automatically.

"I beg your pardon?" I say. My eyes are squinting as if that would clear my ears so I could hear right.

They all look at me like *I'm* the one who's got the problem. I have this urge to burst out laughing. But I suppress it because they obviously don't get the joke. Which actually makes it all the more funny. Okay, so some parts of my trip are actually going to be amusing.

But my amusement fades as another guy comes up to us. He's got dark brown hair that matches his eyes. And he's tall, bronzed, and wearing no shirt. He has jeans hugging those slender hips of his, a washboard stomach, and by every measure he's just about the toughest looking teenager I've ever seen.

"*Americayit,*" Moron says, pointing to me.

No-shirt guy says some stuff to Doo-Doo, Moron, and O'dead in Hebrew and ignores me completely. Which just proves one of my many theories . . . the gorgeous guys are always the biggest jerks. At least the other guys smiled and introduced themselves. No-shirt guy just barks some words at his friends, then walks away.

"How long are you visiting for?" Moron asks, eyeing the suitcases in the back seat.

For a helluva lot longer than I want to. "The whole summer."

"We're going to hang out at the beach tomorrow tonight. Do you want to join us?" Doo-Doo asks.

"Sure," I say.

I look over at the house and there's a crowd of four strangers plus Ron standing in the open doorway. They're all staring at me. How could I have forgotten why I was here in the first place?

Ron walks up to me. I want to ask, "How did it go?" but don't.

So now I find myself walking up this muddy pathway, to this small house that's going to be my residence for the next three months. As the cherry on top of the cake called my life, I'm going to live with family members who I've never met before and a biological father who I hardly know.

"Amy, this is my *brudder*, Chaim."

My uncle holds out his hand and shakes mine. He's a tall guy with a definite resemblance to Ron. They both have that same strong, muscular build.

The guy is smiling, but I can tell there's tension behind that façade. Anger, too, although I don't know if it's directed at me or SD (short for Sperm Donor, I'm too hot and sweaty to think of him as anything other than SD).

"Call me *Dod* or Uncle Chaim," he says.

As if I could even say that name. He pronounces the C-h like he's about to hack a loogie. I swear I can't do those back throat noises for the life of me without making a complete ass of myself. I'll just call him Uncle Chime and leave off the gurgling back-throat noise.

The lady beside Uncle Chime steps forward. I'm shocked when she pulls me to her and hugs me tightly. My first instinct is to push her away, but her embrace is so warm and loving. I find myself leaning into her arms. She releases me after a long time, puts her hands on my shoulders, and holds me at arm's length.

"Beautiful girl," she says with a deep Israeli accent.

She has these earrings with bells on them and no makeup on her face. My mom wouldn't be caught dead outside the house without makeup. Or earrings with bells dangling from them. The truth is, this woman is pretty without makeup and the bells just make her look angelic instead of stupid.

She lets go of me and says with a smile, "I'm your aunt Yikara. Just call me *Doda* Yucky, okay?"

"Ookaay," I say in a singsong voice to alert SD I'm not comfortable calling this lady Yucky.

"*Doda* is 'aunt' in Hebrew," SD explains as if that was the part of this whole exchange that needed explanation.

She just asked me to call her yucky!

There are two more people standing there. One is a small boy, probably around three years old, with blond curls spiraling out of his head like Medusa's snakes. He's wearing nothing but a pair of Power Ranger underpants.

"*Shalom*, *ani* Matan," he says in a cute little voice. I have no clue what he's saying, but he's so adorable and his curls bounce on his head as he speaks. I step toward him and shake his little hand affectionately.

The last one, a dirty blonde-haired teenager who is a bit taller than me, just stands there with her arms crossed over her chest. She's wearing the tightest jeans I've ever seen on a human being and a crop shirt showing most of her flat stomach. I don't need a sixth sense to know she's royally pissed-off.

"This is your cousin, O'snot."

This time my laugh just comes out without warning. Although when I come to my senses and realize nobody else is laughing, I stop pretty quick. Okay, now O'snot is not just pissed-off, she's got *my* famous, one-of-a-kind sneer down pat as if she'd invented it herself.

I don't hold out my hand in greeting because I'm pretty sure my snotty cousin will ignore it. So I just say, "Hi."

"Hi," she says through gritted teeth. Nice.

"Let's go inside so you can meet your *Safta*," Uncle Chime says.

I'm getting a little piece of satisfaction when I notice Ron's armpits are wet through his shirt. My armpit wet spots are the size of grapefruits, but Ron's are the size of small watermelons. He's more nervous than I am for me to meet my grandmother.

Ha!

6

*You can run from some problems,
but then you get caught up in others.*

I enter the house slowly and peer inside. A kitchen is right in front of me. I follow Ron to the left and find a woman sitting on a rocking chair next to a window. She has white hair massively peppered with dark strands.

She looks at me with bright blue eyes that almost glow. Our gazes meet and I feel like I'm looking in the mirror at my own eyes. I'm so overwhelmed it almost chokes me. Is the air getting thicker?

I start breathing heavier, trying to get air into my constricting lungs.

My Grandma.

My sick Grandma.

She looks small and weak. Is she dying?

Turning to the rest of the family, I realize they're all staring at me. It makes me feel like I'm being judged on some reality show they're watching. An over-excited television announcer's voice in my head says, *Will Amy make a mistake and screw up this first meeting? Watch next week's episode of Illegitimate Children and find out if her sick grandmother accepts or rejects her in front of thirty million viewers . . .*

Before I even realize it, I turn and run out of the house before anyone can see the tears welling in my eyes. I run and run and run until my legs want to give out. I'm passing rows of houses, haystacks, horses, cows, and sheep as if I'm on some kind of farm set in Hollywood.

When I stop running and start walking, I think *Safta* must think I'm some stupid idiot. I meant to hug her, I really did. But not in front the rest of the family. I feel like they're analyzing my every move.

I keep walking, pissed at SD for making my first meeting with *Safta* a spectacle. A small wire fence is in front of me, and as I attempt to step over it, a voice stops me.

"You can't go there."

I freeze and turn to the harsh voice. It's no-shirt guy standing in front of a pile of hay about three stories tall. A sheen of sweat on his chest sparkles in the sunshine, but I'm trying not to pay attention to it. Instead, I think about something gross. Like how he must smell like sheep and sweat and how he's in desperate need of a shower. But, for that matter, so am I. I wipe the tears falling down my cheek with my fingertips.

"Isn't this a free country?" I say with attitude.

The last thing I need is for some hard-ass teenager to think I'm weak.

He turns around and flings a whole bale of hay into the sheep pens.

"The sign says a minefield is behind the fence. If you want to take your chances, I won't stop you," no-shirt-cute-jerk says as he enters the sheep enclosure.

At this point I'm still straddling the fence. Damn. This IS a war zone. I eye my foot on the other side of the wire, feeling lucky it's still there and not blown off. I slowly lift it and bring it back to the side of the wire without minefields.

"You don't know where you are, do you?" he asks gruffly as he gets another bale of hay.

"Sure I do," I say. "I'm on top of a mountain in the middle of Israel." Duh.

"Actually, you're in the northern part of Israel, not in the middle. In the Golan Heights."

"So?"

"Americans," he mumbles, then slowly shakes his head in disgust.

"Okay, what's so special about the Golan Heights?"

"Let's just say Syria is about ten miles that way," he says, pointing. "For a Jewish girl, you don't know much about the Jewish homeland."

Yeah, but I'm not Jewish. I don't tell him this, he'll probably go off on me about it. I'm glad when he turns away and walks back into the sheep enclosure.

"Arg!"

I jump at the sound at my feet. A mangy, dirt-encrusted puppy, who I think at one time was white, is furiously wagging his tail at me. Once we make eye contact, he rolls onto his back and puts his paws in the air.

"I'm sorry," I say to the mutt. "I'm not a dog person."

Go find some other sucker to rub their hands on that filthy, flea-ridden tummy of yours. I'm not a cat person, either. In fact, I'm not an animal person at all. And being surrounded by a farmload of the things is making me itch.

I start to walk away. Unfortunately, the mutt follows.

"Arg!" the thing says again.

I keep walking.

"Don't you know dogs say 'ruff,' not 'arg'?" I ask it. "What are you trying to be, a pirate?"

The dog answers with another, "Arg!" this time screechier than the last as if he's trying to annoy me on purpose. Hey, the way my day has been going, I wouldn't doubt it.

"Ruff! Ruff! Ruff!"

You'd think the mutt was joking with me, wouldn't you? But as I turn to the rough, deep barking sound I realize pretty quickly the mutt has friends. A lot of them.

In the first place, I was wrong about it being dirt-encrusted. These five dogs are caked in mud and definitely dirtier than the mutt-puppy. Also (in the first place) they're very, very big.

And they're running right toward me barking up a storm as if I'd kidnapped their child.

Panic isn't the word to describe how I feel right now. As my life flashes before my eyes, I briefly weigh my two options. I could either head toward the wire and run into the minefields or jump into the sheep pens.

I don't have time to waste so I just run as fast as my sweaty, tired, sorry legs can carry me. As I move, I'm not even conscious about which option I've chosen.

I run faster and faster, barely aware of the high-pitched "arg" sound at my feet and the hefty "ruffs" not far behind. Just a little farther, I say to my clouded mind. I think I'm screaming and yelling obscenities, but I can't be sure because I'm too busy worrying about what my legs are doing and can't be bothered with censoring my mouth, too.

It seems like a long time, but when I reach the enclosure my pace doesn't falter. Mr. Haraldson, my gym teacher, would be proud of my leap. I was nowhere near getting the presidential award in physical fitness last year, but I'm probably making a world-record jump right now.

I don't really aim where I'm going; it's all just a blur. And when I land, I close my eyes. I hope I don't squash a sheep during my crash landing.

But instead of colliding with a sheep, something hard and solid breaks my fall.

I'm afraid to open my eyes, so I can't see, but my sense of smell is heightened. I know this because the scent of boy sweat surrounds me.

It's not grody body odor, just this musky guy aroma that makes me inhale deeper.

Okay, now I realize what I'm doing, where I am, and who I'm smelling—like he's a damn rose petal—but it's really just a boy. I open my eyes wide.

Don't ask me how I came to be straddling no-shirt-cute-jerk. His hands are on me. To be specific, one of them is on the small of my back and the other one is on my hip. And I get caught staring into mocha eyes that could definitely put someone in a trance.

I'm about to push away from him, but I hear the sound of someone walking along the grass beside the sheep's pen. I look over at who it is. I'm acutely aware the position I'm currently in looks really promiscuous and will probably get me in a ton of trouble.

When I finally lean away from him, it opens my view to whoever has witnessed my debacle. I realize it's the last person I wanted to see.

O'snot.

And when I see her lips in a tight line and her hands accusingly on her hips I come to the only conclusion one can muster.

No-shirt-cute-jerk is my cousin O'snot's boyfriend.

O'shit.

7

---

*I'll never get used to
being humiliated.*

"I swear, Ron, it's not my fault."

"Those words come off your lips pretty often, Amy," he says to me. "Now explain again why you ran away before you even met *Safta* and then, within a matter of fifteen minutes, end up on top of a boy. In the middle of a pile of hay, no less."

I dig some dirt out of my fingernail while the Sperm Donor has this very serious talk.

"Actually, to be technical, I fell on him," I say. I finger a piece of my hair that's been caked with mud. "I really don't recall exactly how I ended up straddling him."

We're sitting on the front lawn of my grandmother/uncle/aunt/cousin's house. Ron does that thing with his hand through his hair again.

And then unending silence. Should I explain what happened? I'm not afraid to admit I want to be in control of my life.

Don't ask me why, I just blurt out, "I felt like everybody was watching and analyzing me and it sucked so I ran."

"Did you kiss Avi?"

"Who's Avi?"

SD gives me the you've-got-to-be-kidding look.

I stand up.

"No! Why? Did Cousin Snotty say I did? Listen, there were vicious dogs chasing me—"

He looks down at the mutt who hasn't figured out my feet aren't his personal playground.

"Like that one?" he says.

I shake the thing off my leg. "No. Yes. Well, they looked like him, but were a lot bigger. And so I ran and sort of fell on Snotty's boyfriend."

"Her name is O. S. N. A. T. Osnat. It's a beautiful name."

"Not where I come from."

"Just . . . just give her a chance. Don't judge her before you get to know her."

I want to argue, to tell SD Snotty hated *me* before she knew me, but I'm keeping silent. Right now I'll attribute my lack of ability to argue to sleep deprivation because usually I'm ready for a good knockdown-dragout verbal war.

"Fine," I say.

"And stop calling her Snotty."

Geez, you give the guy a little and like a vacuum cleaner he wants to take up all the dirt, not just the little pieces of lint.

"Fine. Where's *Safta*? I'm ready to meet her now if there aren't any spectators around."

"She's resting in her room. No spectators, I promise."

This would be about the time I have the urge to hug the SD. But it would feel weird because I haven't hugged him in years.

SD stands and I follow him into the house. Once we enter, the smell of fresh baked bread wafting from the kitchen makes my stomach growl.

"Come eat," *Doda* Yucky says. She's lost a bit of her cheery disposition. Is it because she thinks I kissed O.S.N.A.T's boyfriend?

"Thanks, but I'm not hungry." I'm too nervous to eat. Ron leads me to a small room at the back of the house and I peek in the door.

Safta is lying down on her bed. When she sees me enter, she sits up.

I swallow hard and close the door behind me. The room is small, the floor is made of tile, and the walls are stark white cement. The drapes are closed, so it's a little dark. But that's the way I want it now, because I don't want the world peeking into my conversation.

"Hi, *Safta*. I'm Amy," I say. My voice cracks while I'm saying it and I feel a little foolish.

She nods and pats the side of the bed. "Come over here, Amy. Sit with me."

I take small, slow steps to her bed. When I reach it, I carefully sit on the edge. To my surprise, she takes my hand in hers.

"Are you really sick?" I ask tentatively.

"I'll be fine. You know doctors, they like to make a big fuss about nothing."

"Ron thinks you're real sick," I say, and then want to suck those words right back in my mouth.

She shakes her head. "Your father needs to have his *cup* examined. That means 'head' in Yiddish. Imagine, keeping my granddaughter from me for sixteen years."

"Yeah," I say, urging her on. I like *Safta* immediately.

"What's your mother like?" she asks, changing the subject.

How do I describe Mom?

"She's pretty, for a mom," I say. "And she has a job that pays her a lot of money. She doesn't have a lot of friends, though, 'cause she's always working."

I watch as *Safta* takes this all in.

"And tell me about yourself."

"I do okay in school, I guess. My best friend's name is Jessica . . . she's Jewish," I add to make some connection to *Safta* on the religious end. "And I like to play tennis, ski, and shop."

She nods her head. "I'm going to like getting to know you, Amy. You sound like a very energetic, interesting girl."

"I should add I don't have the most positive attitude," I say while biting my bottom lip nervously. I mean, the lady'll figure it out sooner or later so I might as well give it to her straight up front.

"Maybe your trip here will change that."

I highly doubt it but I say, "I guess so," just to make her think this trip might miraculously change my outlook on life.

"I was like you when I was your age," she says.

"Why? Were you illegitimate, too?"

"No," she says, still holding my hand. "But my family fell on some tough times and we didn't have a home for a few years."

"Where did you live?"

"On the beach. It was a long time ago. Life changes when you least expect it."

As this information sinks into my brain, *Safta* tells me to go relax and unpack. And she smiles at me as if she's been my grandmother forever.

I can't keep blaming her for not being there for me the past sixteen years. The poor woman didn't even know I existed.

"Where's my suitcase?" I ask Ron after my enlightening talk with *Safta*.

"It's in O'snot's room," he says.

I didn't just hear right. I couldn't have. "You're kiddin' me, right?"

"There's only a few rooms here," SD explains. "You'll be sleeping in O'snot's room. I'm getting the sofa."

"What about the little guy?"

"Matan? He sleeps on a bed in his parents' room."

I'm about to suggest I sleep on the floor, but I see three ants crawling across the tile. Gross. And when I look over at *Doda* Yucky, she has this pathetic look on her face as if she'll win the lottery if my happy meter reaches a certain level.

I give her a little smile and it apparently worked because she heads back to the kitchen humming a cheerful tune.

But seriously, if there's one thing an American teenage girl needs, it's privacy. Can I tell O'snot to leave the room? It is, in fact, HER room so I think not. Thank goodness I'm not a twin. There are these twins at my school, Marlene and Darlene, and they have to not only share a room with each other, but their older sister, Charlene too. Don't ask.

SD leads me to a bedroom in the back of the house. I walk in the room and Snotty is putting on makeup while sitting on her bed. She knows I'm there, but she hasn't acknowledged me.

The Sperm Donor stands beside me. "Do you need help?"

"No, I'm fine," I say back to him.

He takes this as his cue to leave. I would have liked him to stay. Only to pose as a buffer between me and Snotty.

"Listen, I'm sorry about your boyfriend," I say.

She looks up and I see she's overdone the makeup on her eyes. It's as if she's outlined her eyes in black charcoal and now my cousin looks like she's in her twenties instead of a teenager. How old is she, anyway? She could use a few tips on makeup application.

5 1613 00368 4233

51

CALUMET CITY PUBLIC LIBRARY

One of my mom's clients is a cosmetic company. They actually used me in one of the shoots for their teen line. I learned a lot about how makeup should enhance your best features and not look all gloppy and dark (like Snotty). After my picture appeared in most of the teen magazines, my group of friends kind of dubbed me the guru of makeup.

I go over to my suitcase on the bed I suppose is mine for the next three months and pick out some clothes to change into that aren't caked with mud and straw.

"Avi isn't my boyfriend."

I'm not sure if it's Snotty talking, or my imagination playing with me.

I face my cousin. "What?"

She points her charcoal eye-circle bull's-eyes in my direction. "I don't have a boyfriend."

I take a pair of red shorts out of my suitcase. The word BITCH is printed across the butt in big white letters. Jessica got me the shorts for my birthday as a joke along with an anklet that wasn't a joke. I never thought I'd ever wear the shorts but then again, I never thought I'd find myself on a farm on top of a mountain in the middle of a war zone.

But, to be perfectly honest with myself, Israel doesn't actually feel or look like a war zone. Well, except for the heavily armed guards at the airport and the minefield I stepped on.

I look down at my shorts. I didn't think anyone here would be able to speak English so I packed them. I'm tempted to offer them to Snotty but instead ask, "Does Avi have a girlfriend?"

Okay, now if I wouldn't gag from the grossness of it, I'd insert my foot into my mouth. I don't care whether the guy has a girlfriend or not, but here I am asking Snotty about him.

Sometimes my mouth gets me going in a direction I have no intention of heading.

What's worse is my cousin ignores my question. So even if I didn't mean to ask the question, I'm more curious than ever to know the answer. But I'd never give her the satisfaction of asking her about Avi twice. She's already been spreading false rumors I've been mashing with the guy. It would suck if she really thought I cared what his girlfriend status was.

I set my clothes out on the bed, and head for the ONE bathroom in the whole house. I'm trying not to think about living for the next three months in a house with seven people and one bathroom. Scary, isn't it? At home we have three bathrooms . . . and it's only me and mom living there (along with Marc with a "c" when he stays over).

I have this friend, Emily. She's obsessed with smelling EVERYTHING. Like, when she eats she smells each bite before she puts the food into her mouth. I hate having meals with her because every time I hear her sniff-eat-sniff-eat-sniff-eat I get extremely irritated. Nobody really likes me when I'm irritated, except maybe Jessica.

As I enter the bathroom, my gag meter indicates low readings of any smells other than the ones emanating from my own body. Man, Emily would have a field day with me.

I am SO looking forward to getting clean. Thinking about how long it's been since I took a shower is making me dizzy.

I close the door to the bathroom and look on the handle for a lock. But the problem is there isn't one. Just a hole, as if there was a lock at one point in time.

This isn't funny. There are seven people living in this house and no lock on the bathroom door. And the damn door has a peephole where a lock should be.

I need to get into bed fast so this day can be over. I don't want to undress in front of a peephole so I step into the tub, close the curtain, and take my clothes off. I figure out how to turn on the water.

Thankfully a spray of hot water comes hard and fast. I can't stop the moan from escaping my mouth. Hot showers rock. I'm so tired I can hardly stand so I quickly wash myself.

After the shower I head back to Snotty's room, wondering why I didn't bring a change of clothes with me to the bathroom-that-doesn't-lock. I sure as hell don't want to change in front of Snotty. As I'm thinking about where to change into pjs, I wrap the towel tightly around myself.

I don't want to make eye contact with her, 'cause I want to avoid having to make any positive facial gestures, like smiling. I don't have any positive facial gestures left, at least not any today. In fact, all my positive gestures are probably used up for tomorrow, too.

So I look down at the floor as I enter the room, close the door, and head straight for my suitcase. I know Snotty is still in the room, I can hear her breathing. I pull a tank top and underwear out of my suitcase. I can go back to the bathroom and feel like a big dork that I'm embarrassed to change in front of her or I can just suck it up and change right here with my back turned.

I drop the towel and put my underwear on. Then I put on the BITCH shorts. When I reach for my white tank top, the door opens. I quickly cover my large breasts with my tank and get ready to yell at the intruder. The intruder, I assume, is none other than SD. "Do you mind?" I say.

But the person who walks into the room is not SD. It's Snotty. Which means there's someone else on her bed. I whip my head around and find Avi sitting there.

"Aaaahhhhhh!" I scream at the top of my lungs.

Avi just had a very big peep show starring yours truly.

Unfortunately my scream only alerts SD and Uncle Chime, who come barging into the room. SD's eyes dart back and forth between Avi and the half-dressed me with the BITCH shorts on.

"What's going on in here?" SD barks, accusing me with his eyes.

Avi actually saw me undressed . . . my butt, my boobs, my cellulite thighs. My tongue is in shock, just like the rest of me. Even if I could talk, I wouldn't even know what to say.

Except I smell a rat.

I look at Snotty, who has this very subtle self-satisfied smirk on her face. She's the rat, no question about it.

Uncle Chime is eyeing Ron accusingly. I know I didn't do anything, but I feel like a *ho* nonetheless.

Out of the corner of my eye I notice Avi standing up. He says something in Hebrew to SD I can't understand.

Ron says something angrily back to him.

Snotty starts arguing with Ron.

Uncle Chime stands as straight as a soldier, blocking the door, his hands on his hips.

And I'm just standing here, half naked. I push past Uncle Chime and run to the bathroom. After I put on my tank, I still hear loud arguing coming from Snotty's room.

I sit on the edge of the bathtub until the arguing stops.

If this is my initiation to Israel, I'm scared to find out what the next three months here are going to be like.

8

You can attract bees with honey,
but why would you want to?

The jet lag excuse works like a dream on the Sperm Donor
my second day in Israel, with the added benefit that I've
been able to sleep most of the day.

But now it's the late afternoon and I'm fully rested.
After grabbing a bite to eat, I put on my jogging outfit,
grab my iPod, and head outside. As I venture down the
street, I spot *Safta* sitting outside on a lounge chair on the
edge of the mountain.

When she notices me, she waves me over.

I jog down the dirt road and stand next to her. Peering
down the mountain, at the lake far below, and at the other
mountains in the distance takes my breath away. "Chicago
is as flat as . . ." I'm about to say "Snotty," but I don't.

Instead, I say, "We don't have any mountains where I live. I guess that's why they make skyscrapers, they're like Chicago's mountains."

"I've never been to Chicago," *Safta* says.

"Well, you'll have to come visit me. I can take you to the Sears Tower. You can see, like, four states from the top floor. It's totally cool. And we have Lake Michigan. It's so wide you can't even see across it."

I get excited thinking about taking her around Chicago when she comes to visit me. She will love Millennium Park, where she can watch people and have lunch on the grass smack dab in the middle of the city.

And I bet she'll love the Art Institute of Chicago and Museum of Science and Industry. The museum has awesome exhibits. My favorite is the dead baby exhibit.

It's really called the Neonatal exhibit, but I say just tell it like it is. It's a bunch of real, dead babies of every stage, all encased in formaldehyde or some other liquid. They have about thirty embryos and fetuses that are one week old on up to a full term baby. They even show identical twin embryos. It's the coolest thing I've ever seen.

Yeah, it would be neat to have *Safta* come visit.

I sigh, getting caught up in the moment. "I feel like I could scan the whole country from up here." Then I think about the malls, miles and miles from here. "But it's so far from everything."

"You're a city girl, eh?"

"Through and through. Give me a Kate Spade purse and a pair of Lucky jeans and I'm a happy girl."

She laughs, the soft, warm sound filling the air.

"I love it here. Away from the noise, away from crowds. It's the perfect place on earth for an old woman like me. Besides, at my age I don't need a Kate Spade purse or Lucky jeans."

"I'm sure you were one hot mama when you were a teenager," I say, then want to take those words right back. Talking to her like she's one of my friends is a stupid thing to do.

"I married your grandfather when I was eighteen years old."

"Was it love at first sight?"

"No. I couldn't stand the sight of him. Until one day he bought me flowers."

Flowers? That's the oldest trick in the book. "So he brought you some roses and you fell in love?" It's a cute story, if a little boring.

Safta pats my hand. "No, *motek*. He bought me the whole flower shop. And the poor man was allergic to pollen."

"Wow." I'd be sold if a guy bought me my own Abercrombie and Fitch store. Now, that would be true love.

Safta starts to get up, and I grab her elbow to help her. Even though she told me she's fine, I have a feeling I'm not getting the whole story.

"I'm going to lie down," she says once she stands. "Go explore the moshav, your father should be back with dinner soon." I watch as she walks back down the dirt path toward the house.

Taking a deep breath, I head toward the entrance to the moshav. The winding road will be a great place for me to take a jog.

As I reach the security booth, a guy sticks his head out of the window.

"I'm going for a run," I say.

He nods his head and opens the gate.

When I start to jog, the fresh air in my lungs energizes me. The mountainous view is like out of a movie, and the music in my ears reminds me of home. I'm in heaven as my stride matches the rhythm of the song I'm listening to.

If only Mitch could see me now, jogging down a mountain. He's a nature nut. My best friend Jessica is, too. She'd probably be jealous of me.

While I'm thinking of Mitch and Jess, I whiz past some white boxes. Only after I pass them do I realize what they are.

Beehives.

What the hell are beehives doing on the side of the road?

I think I'm safe, until I see one of the stinging suckers has followed me. "Go away," I say, running faster. The bee flies faster, and he's doing circles around me.

I stop and stand as still as those guards in London who stand at the palace, hoping that will make him go away. But it doesn't, it only attracts another bee. And another. And another.

It feels like time has stopped, except my iPod is still playing music in my ear.

"Help!" I scream, and take off again. I'm waving my arms around like a madwoman, trying to get the bees off of me. Gross, I think one just got caught in my hair!

I'm running.

And waving my arms.

And shaking my head.

When I spot a car coming up the road, I'm hopeful it's Ron. But I'm shaking my head around so hard that I don't see who it is. The car passes me, but then I hear tires screech.

I run toward the car, until I realize who's getting out of the driver's side.

Avi.

The last possible person in the world I want to see.

"Get in," he says, opening up the passenger side.

I have two options: get in the car with a jerk who saw me buck naked or get stung by seven bees.

Call me crazy, call me stupid. But I choose option number two. "Go to hell," I say, and keep running down the mountain.

About three-quarters of the way down, the bees finally leave me alone. By some miracle, I've managed to avoid getting stung.

But now I'm stuck at the bottom of the mountain. And I don't want to go back up and pass the beehives again.

I have a brilliant idea. I'll wait for the Sperm Donor. *Safta* said he'll be coming back soon.

So I wait. And wait.

Forty-five minutes later, I'm still waiting.

I swear, this vacation is a total disaster. If I were home, I'd be playing tennis and hanging out with friends.

An hour goes by before I spot a car coming up the road. I recognize Doo-Doo. I wave my arms in the air like an air traffic control guy to make him stop. There's a girl in the car with him. The girl sticks her head out the window. "Do you need a ride?"

"Uh, yeah."

"Get inside."

Doo-Doo introduces me to the girl as I hop in the back seat. Her name is Ofra, and she also lives on the moshav. I lean back and enjoy the air conditioning blasting in the car.

"O'dead says you're going to come to the beach with us tonight." Ofra turns around and faces me from the front seat. "It's a special occasion."

"Your birthday?" I guess.

"No. Moron is going to the army."

That's something to celebrate?

Ofra looks excited when she says, "You have to bring something of yours to give him, then offer a piece of advice. It's the *moshav* ritual."

Ritual?

I think I'm allergic to rituals.

9

*Before you speak up, make sure you
know what you're saying.*

The beach we go to is sandy, and borders a huge lake they
tell me is called the Kineret. It's all seven of us tonight: me,
Ofra, Snotty, Avi, Moron, Doo-Doo, and O'dead. The guys
have made a huge bonfire, and we're sitting around it.

Avi leads Moron to a chair he's placed in the sand.
Then he pulls out a shirt from a bag with Hebrew letters
ironed on it. When he holds it up, everyone laughs.

Except me, of course, because I have no clue what's
written on the shirt.

"What does it say?" I ask Ofra.

"Where's the bathroom?" she says.

"I don't know," I say. "I guess you're going to have to
wait or pee in the sand."

They all laugh harder. And I realize they're laughing at me. "What?" I say.

Ofra pats my back. "I wasn't asking you where the bathroom is, I was telling you that's what the shirt says."

Oh, man.

"Avi, speak in English so Amy can understand," Ofra says.

He stands there, totally intimidating. "*Beseder*," he says begrudgingly. "My friend Moron here has gotten us lost on many occasions. His sense of direction is legendary, to say the least. So with this shirt, he might not be able to find his way home, but he'll be able to find his way to the nearest *sheruteem*." Then he looks at me and says, "That means bathroom."

Everyone else chuckles and claps.

"And my piece of advice is . . . don't flirt with any of the female instructors. They all have access to weapons bigger than yours."

This amuses everyone. I assume Moron has a reputation for flirting with girls.

After Avi sits down, Ofra and Snotty go up to Moron and give him a wrapped present. He opens it and holds a pair of boxer shorts up to us.

The front is just plain white, but ironed to the back is a map of Israel. "This way," Snotty says, "when you get lost you can always find your way back home."

"Yeah, but he's got to get naked to see the map," Doo-Doo says, laughing.

I laugh, too. Imagining Moron stuck in the middle of the desert, lost, wearing a shirt that says *Where's the bathroom* while he's naked from the waist down as he examines the map on his boxers, is pretty hysterical.

Ofra sits on one of Moron's legs, and Snotty sits on the other. "Our piece of advice is . . . let us shave your head instead of the army hairdresser."

I watch as Ofra pulls a cordless razor out of a bag. Moron gives a nervous smile to the rest of us. To be honest, he has a great head of hair. It's sandy brown, almost reaches his shoulders, and is really thick. Is he gonna let them shave it off?

Ofra turns on the razor, then she and Snotty stand up and go behind him.

"Take your shirt off," Doo-Doo suggests.

Moron pulls his shirt over his head, then raises his eyebrows. "Be gentle with me, girls," he teases.

"Keep your pants on," Ofra jokes and everyone, including me, laughs.

Snotty makes the first stripe down the middle of Moron's head as he squints his eyes shut.

O'dead takes a picture just as Snotty finishes one line. Then Ofra takes the razor and makes another stripe. They're all having a good time. Even, dare I admit it, me.

"Give Amy a turn," Doo-Doo suggests, then gives me a little push of encouragement.

I shake my head. "I'm not great with a razor," I say. Especially electric ones next to people's scalps.

Ofra and Snotty finish shaving Moron's head. They're having fun making designs with his hair as they do the job.

After they're done, O'dead stands next to Moron. "We've been friends since we were three, and I know how scared you are of the dark." O'dead pulls out a small flashlight. "So now, when they stick you in the Negev desert, you won't have anything to fear."

"Except the deadly snakes," Doo-Doo chimes in, making everyone laugh again.

"As long as I have females in my unit," Moron says, "I won't need any light, if you know what I mean."

"Which brings me to *my* gift," Doo-Doo says, then pulls out a small, pink, stuffed teddy bear. "This is for you to sleep with when you're alone at night and need something to hug."

"Our piece of advice is . . . when you sleep with your gun, make sure the safety is on."

Moron nods his head. "Great advice, guys."

"Now it's Amy's turn," Ofra says.

I look over at Snotty. The girl won't even acknowledge me. Then I turn to Ofra. "Go ahead," she says, urging me with her hand to get up.

Tentatively, I walk over to Moron and hold out a piece of material. "It's a bandana," I explain. "With a peace sign on it."

He takes the material from my hand and studies it. "*Todah*, thank you."

"They told me I should give you a piece of advice, too," I say. Then I clear my throat. Everyone is looking at me, even Snotty. And it makes me feel all sweaty inside. Talk about pressure.

"My piece of advice is . . ."

I swear, I had something to say, but forgot it. I'm on the spot here and my mind draws a blank. Shit. I look at the horizon, where the sun is falling into the water. The first thing that comes into my mind and out of my mouth is, "don't swim on a full stomach."

Oh my God. I can't believe I just said that. The guy is going to the desert for basic training. What are the chances that he's going to be swimming in the middle of the desert during military training?

My advice is met with silence.

"That was very . . . deep, Amy," Snotty says, clearly making fun of me.

I hear Doo-Doo ask O'dead, "Is she joking?"

If I knew how to get back to the moshav, I'd run there right now without turning back. But I can't, so I sit back down and try and shrink as much as I can into the sand.

"Well, I guess I should say something," Moron says, then stands. "Thank you for this great party, the gifts, and advice. Your friendship means a lot to me. Now, I know you're supposed to throw me into the Kineret, but you better not even try it."

"You have to get wet," Avi says matter-of-factly, gesturing toward the lake.

Doo-Doo and O'dead are ready to back Avi as he chases Moron around the beach.

I'm shocked when they tackle him and throw him into the water, making a huge splash. Moron is soaking wet, but he's not pissed. I would be if my friends tossed me, clothes and all, into a lake. But he's laughing right along with the rest of them.

Ofra goes to help Moron out of the water, until he grabs her arm and pulls her in with him.

Snotty joins the group. I watch as she puts her arms around Avi, and they both splash in the water together.

Hel-*lo*. Don't these people know it's usually the custom to swim with bathing suits, not fully clothed? Of course I'm not jealous they're in the water, laughing and having fun. I am absolutely content to stand here all alone.

"Amy, join us!" Moron calls out to me.

"Yeah," Ofra says. "The water's great."

I'm a land person, and don't particularly love water. "No, thanks," I say.

The first one out of the lake is my cousin. She stands straight in front of the bonfire, warming herself. I try to avoid making eye contact with her—I'm afraid if I do my mouth might get me in trouble.

But maybe I should try, like Ron said, to get to know her. Even though she's been rude, it could be because she doesn't know what a great and fun person I am. I guess I really haven't given her much of a chance. I'll attempt to soften her up a bit first. "Osnat, I really enjoyed meeting your friends," I say, thinking of how Ron said her name is spelled.

I swear, I deserve a medal for being so nice. She's probably going to say how much she's glad I opened up the lines of communication. Maybe by the end of the summer she'll be like the sister I never had.

My wayward thoughts are squashed as I watch her turn to me with a toss of her hair and say, "Just remember, Amy. They're my friends, not yours."

And just like that she goes back to being Snotty.

10

*Sometimes we have to prove to others
we're strong even when we're not.*

I've been in Israel for three weeks now.

Thankfully, I'm able to avoid Snotty and Avi. That
means I'm spending a lot of time in the house with *Safta*,
which is just fine with me.

She relayed stories about when she was a kid here in
Israel and more about my grandfather, who died before I
was born. She also told me about her parents, who escaped
from Germany during World War II. Learning about my
extended family has opened my eyes to another world.

As I wake up one morning to Ron's cheery, "Rise and
shine, sleepyhead," I just want to go back to sleep.

What time is it anyway?

SD's words are buzzing around in my head like one of those bees that wouldn't leave me alone. I glance at my watch.

"Six thirty!" I say with a groggy voice. "Please have a very good reason why you're waking me before the sun shines through that window."

Now I know I'm being crabby, but I'm just not a morning person. Never have been, never will be. In my opinion, six thirty isn't even morning; it's still the middle of the night.

"Amy, we've been here a while now and I've left you alone. If you keep sleeping all day, you'll never get over your jet lag. Besides, work needs to be done around here and everyone pitches in. I want you to at least act like you're my daughter and help out."

I sit up and say, "Listen, I'm still tired and cranky. Just come back in, let's say, a couple of hours and we can discuss whatever you want."

"You're always tired and cranky and you need to get out of bed so Yucky can wash the sheets. There's probably mushrooms growing on them."

"Very funny."

"I've promised to help your uncle sell some of the sheep these next few weeks. After that, I want to show you my country."

"Yeah, let's do that. In a couple of weeks," I say just so he'll leave me alone.

I lie back down and pull the covers over my head. A little more sleep is what I need, not to work on my summer vacation or go sightsee. I'll have to convince the

Sperm Donor just because I happen to be on this stupid trip doesn't mean I have to do anything on it.

I let out a breath when I hear him leave the room. Looking over at Snotty's bed, I see it's empty. She's probably over at Avi's house.

Not that I'm jealous, 'cause I'm not. I just don't know why he's friends with her. She might be pretty, but she's mean.

Or maybe she's just mean to me. Which makes me hate her even more.

I close my eyes and try to think about good things, like going back home.

Nothing really makes me happy now. Is that what being sixteen is all about? If so, I can understand why teenagers express themselves in so many different ways. It's not as if we're stupid, we're just trying to figure out where we fit.

Me? I don't seem to fit anywhere these days. I'm like a square peg trying to fit into a round society. Now that I think about it more, I'm not square or round. More like an octagon. And I don't fit anywhere now. I thought I did, but my nice, super-dictated world has complicated all that. I wonder how Mitch is doing without me. Does he miss me?

I fall asleep again and when I wake up my stomach growls so I head to the kitchen. Everyone is gone and the house is quiet.

I glance over at *Safta*, who's sitting in a velour chair reading some book.

"*Boker tov*, Amy," she says in this dignified voice as I reach into the refrigerator and scan the contents.

"I'm sorry," I say. "I don't know what that means."

I finally learned *shalom* means three things: hello, goodbye, and peace. My Hebrew knowledge is pathetic, at best.

"*Boker tov* means 'good morning.'"

"Oh. *Boker tov* to you, too."

Gram seems a little quiet this morning. I'll sit with her and chitchat while I eat breakfast, maybe that'll cheer her up. In fact, I'll prepare something special for her.

As I arrange a plate of fruit, I take my time and cut little pieces of banana and melon in these shapes Jessica's mom taught me. Jessica calls things people rave about "crowd pleasers." Little cut-up fruit in the shape of a clown face is a definite crowd pleaser.

I set the plate down in front of her on a side table. "*Todah*," she says.

"You're welcome." I look down at my masterpiece. "It's a clown face."

"Very creative. Do you like cooking?"

"Not really. Eating I like. We go to restaurants mostly back home."

"Your father doesn't cook for you?"

I know what you're thinking. This is a great opportunity for me to tell *Safta* how it really is back home. But as I look at the old lady's glowing blue eyes I feel protective of her. As much as I'd like my gram to be ashamed of the Sperm Donor, I just can't make myself upset her.

"Well, every Friday he makes this great lasagna," I say, my mouth moving without my brain thinking too long about it. "And his chicken picatta is out of this world. He even bakes blueberry muffins for me on Sunday mornings."

The ol' lady has this little twinkle in her eye that I can't decipher.

"Chicken picatta, huh?" she says.

Oh, shit. She's onto me. I probably should have left out the muffins or made it BBQ chicken instead of picatta. But I'm stickin' with my story for better or worse.

"Yep. I'm sure if you ask him he'll make you some," I say as I look down at my feet and notice my toenail polish is chipped.

I hear the door open and *Doda* Yucky comes floating into the house. "Amy, *Safta* is starting her chemotherapy treatment in an hour," she says. We both help my grandma up. "Everyone is with the *sheeps*," *Doda* Yucky says. "They're waiting for you."

I am bowled over by a terrible sense of worry about *Safta*. Chemotherapy? Oh no . . . that means cancer.

"Can I go with you?" I ask. "I can read to you if you'd like."

Safta pats the back of my hand lightly. "Don't worry, I'll be fine. Go with the young people and enjoy your stay here. You don't want to be hanging around a hospital all day. Okay?"

"Okay."

I want to go with her, to make sure the doctors know she's *my Safta* and she needs the best care possible. Do they know how important she is?

Doda Yucky shuffles *Safta* out the door and I'm alone again. I continue to avoid the *sheeps* today. Ron wants me to help, but what if he gives me a job I can't do?

I don't want to give him a reason to resent I'm his kid. And if the opposite happened, if he bragged to everyone how great I am, I don't want the truth to come out that I'm less than perfect.

Deep down, even though we have major issues to overcome, I want him to be proud of me. I know it's a dumb thought, but it's true.

I spend the next hour rearranging my side of the closet. My eye catches on the skimpy clothes on the other side. Snotty sure does like showing a lot of skin.

I walk outside and wouldn't you know the yelping pup is waiting for me at the door. Great, the only one who likes me here is a dog.

"Arg!"

"Dumb mutt," I mutter.

"Arg!"

I ignore the mop following me at my feet. My spirits lift a bit when in front of the house, right under a nice big tree, is a hammock. I maneuver myself into it and put my hands behind my head as a pillow.

"Arg!"

I look in between the holes in the hammock and notice the mutt under me.

"What do you want?" I ask it.

"Arg! Arg! Arg!"

I groan. Dogs aren't my thing. They're really not. But just to shut it up I get off the hammock and pick up the nuisance. I get back on the hammock with the thing in my arms. It has to lay on me because he'd fall through the holes otherwise. He finds a comfortable spot on my stomach and sighs contentedly.

Against my better judgment, I find myself petting him. Even though he probably has fleas and other insects living off his body, he's soft and fluffy, like a down comforter.

"I-me!"

I look down and spot a cherubic face smiling up at me. It's my little cousin, Matan. He can't say my name right, he just calls me I-me. I think it's cute so I don't correct him.

Mutt jumps off my lap and I sit up. I see Matan has collected flowers in his chubby hands, and they're for me. My frozen heart starts to melt as he hands me the yellow, purple, and white wildflowers (or weeds, however you choose to look at them).

His smile widens when I take the flowers from him, smell them, and say, "Mmmm."

It's amazing how little effort it takes to make a child happy. Unfortunately, they all grow up and become cynical sixteen-year-olds like me.

Picking Matan up, I set him on the hammock next to me. He laughs as I swing the thing back and forth. I take one of the flowers and push the stem into his hair, the flower sticking out of his long, curly locks.

"Pretty," I say, laughing.

I know he doesn't understand a word of English, but he laughs back, then takes a flower out of my hand and puts it into *my* hair. We do this for about ten minutes, until we're both full of colorful wildflowers sticking out of our hair.

He speaks Hebrew to me and I speak English back to him. It doesn't matter that we're both oblivious to what the other is saying, we're having fun. And fun is universal in any language.

A lady who I haven't seen before comes up to us and says something to Matan. He jumps off the hammock and runs to her.

"Yucky left him with me, but he wanted to come see you. I hope it was okay," she says.

"It's fine," I say. "What does the name Matan mean in Hebrew?"

She looks down at my little cousin. "It means 'gift,'" she explains before leading him away.

He turns back, runs to me, and gives me a big hug. "*Shalom*, I-me," he says, then bounds off.

I give a little wave. "*Shalom*, Matan."

When he looks back with his hair full of flowers and furiously waves back at me, I realize I've just made my second friend in Israel (Mutt being the first).

11

Don't trust males.
Human or otherwise.

Going into the house, I take out my nail polish and hold
it up. Cotton Candy is the name of the color. It's a bright,
shiny pink that sparkles in the sunlight. I think it'll look
great when the hellish sun reflects off of it.

I decide to paint my nails outside in the sun after I
take the old polish off. Sitting down on the concrete in
front of the house, I open the bottle. I feel better. I guess
doing something I'm used to doing back home helps.

The mutt lies down next to me, using me as his shady
tree. I let him, just because he'll keep bugging me anyway.
I paint my toenails until I hear a sound coming out of the
mutt's butt that sounds surprisingly like a fart.

"Eww," I say.

The dog doesn't get up, he just looks at me like *I'm* bothering *him*.

"Listen, if you're going to hang around me there's a couple of rules. Rule number one: bark like a dog. Rule number two: take a bath before you rub up against me. Rule number three: I don't want a dog, so go find someone else to bug. Rule number four, five, and six: no dog farts. Got it?"

Wouldn't you know it the mutt gets his lazy ass up and walks away. Did I say something wrong? Maybe I should go play with him later. Just so there's no hard feelings.

I go back to painting my nails when I hear someone walk up to the house. I look over and it's Avi, the last guy in the universe I want to see. And he's staring at me.

I dip the brush in the nail polish.

"Why stare? You've already seen me without my clothes on," I say, trying not to look in his direction. It's pretty hard, because he looks like an Abercrombie model.

But then I remember he saw me naked and I want him to be anywhere but in my line of vision. I can't walk because my toenails are wet and I don't want to smudge them. Anyway, why should I be the one to move?

Mutt decides at that moment to come back. I expect him to come directly to me, but instead he hobbles over to Avi.

Traitor.

"I wouldn't touch that thing," I say. "He's dirtier than my Uncle Bob."

Uncle Bob works in a factory. He cleans up okay, but no matter how many times he washes his hands, there's always this black, gooey gunk stuck under his nails.

Avi bends down and pets the traitor, who wags his tail so vigorously you'd think it was a flag in some parade. Then he looks at me. Not the traitor, Avi.

"You're not much for helping, are you?" he says.

I don't even have to try and sneer, his comment makes my lip curl on its own.

"What*ever*," I say.

Then I go back to painting my toenails a second coat. But now I'm so pissed at what Avi said my hand starts shaking and I'm getting nail polish on my toe-skin. Each stroke now looks like a two-year-old kid had a field day with the brush on my toes.

The dog trots over to me and buries his wet nose under my arm.

"Go away," I say.

He won't leave, he just sits down in front of me. I look over at Avi again, who's still eyeing me. Why does he do that?

"Arg!"

"Traitor," I grumble through gritted teeth to the mutt.

"Arg!"

If I tell you what the mutt does next you're not going to believe me. He sticks that butt of his in the air, like he's trying to play with me or something. When I don't take the bait, he grabs my shoe with his teeth and runs away.

Now this isn't just any shoe, it's my one and only pair of Ferragamo jelly sandals.

"Give that back!" I yell. "Do you have any idea how much that cost?"

I try to grab for it, but the white devil-pup starts shaking it back and forth in its mouth like a chew toy.

"Stop it," I say in a loud, warning tone.

But he doesn't. He starts running away with it. I get up, trying not to ruin my still-wet toenails in the process. But it's no use. As I head toward the dog, it trots away in the opposite direction.

Now it's war.

Most of the time I go through life at a relatively slow pace, but that doesn't mean I can't haul ass every once in a while. The only problem is my boobs bob up and down when I run fast. But I try not to think of that. I'm concentrating on saving my Ferragamo sandal.

The mutt stops beside one of the houses and I pretend I'm not going to get it. I sneak behind a lemon tree with the hugest lemons I've ever seen. They're as big as a baby's head.

When I think he might forget I'm behind the tree, I sneak a look at him. His butt is in the air again and his tail is wagging a mile a minute. He's looking straight at me.

And my sandal is still in his mangy, slobbery mouth.

"You should get neutered," I say as I step from behind the tree. Maybe then he'd have some respect for Ferragamo.

"Grrrr."

"What, no 'arg'?" While I'm talking to him, I'm sneaking up to him. "Keep that tail wagging so I can have something to grab at when I catch you, you slimy mutt."

"Grrrr."

"You don't scare me," I continue, inching closer. I'm almost within reach.

"Grrrr."

My concentration is solely on the sandal until I step and feel something squishy squeeze in between my toes. I look down and realize I've just stepped on an old, rotten cucumber. But at second glance, I realize it's not a cucumber, it's a DEAD SNAKE. It's black, but shimmers a bright fluorescent green in the sunlight.

I've never been more grossed out as I am now, running toward my uncle and aunt's house. Obscenities, some I even make up, are streaming out of my mouth. I'm trying hard not to think about the snake-guts that must be in the crevices of my toes as I run as fast as my legs can carry me.

"Ho . . ." I say to Avi in-between gagging. Please dear God let me get the word out before gagging again. "Ho . . ." Gag. "Hose!" I point to my foot just in case he doesn't get it.

The jerk gives a short laugh (at my expense) and I follow him to the back of the house. When I see the hose, I run toward it as fast as my snake-encrusted feet can carry me.

Avi turns the handle and I quickly chance a glance at my gross foot. Little pieces of black, stringy guts are peeking out from in between my toes. My toenails are dry now, with pieces of grass or hay stuck to them permanently.

I'm still gagging, I can't help it. I think if I stop looking at my toes I can get through this. When the water starts spurting out of the hose, I take it from him and aim the water toward my foot. My gaze lands on Avi. "Thanks a lot for helping me get my sandal," I say sarcastically.

"Thanks a lot for helping with the *sheeps*," he counters.

"It's *sheep*, not *sheeps*. Whether you have one sheep or a million of 'em, it's still sheep."

He walks forward and pulls the hose out of my hand. I watch wide-eyed as he bends on one knee and lifts my gross foot and places it in his hand. Then, if you can believe it, he washes my foot thoroughly.

I'm about to lose my balance, I really am. And it's not because I want Avi to catch me or anything. I hate playing the damsel in distress every time he's around.

I'm lightheaded because it's ungodly hot outside and I just busted my ass to run after a Ferragamo-stealing mutt. To top it off, this boy who I'm determined to hate has one of my feet in his hands.

"You can stop gagging. Whatever you stepped in is gone."

"It was a snake!"

He shrugs. Like it's no biggie.

"You ever stepped on a snake?" I ask.

"I usually watch where I step."

I yank my foot out of his grasp. "Well, where I live there are no snakes. Dead or otherwise."

He stands, which is not so great because I was feeling superior when he was on his knee. But he's probably six feet tall and when he looks down at me I feel small. Instead of responding, he gently pulls a flower out of my hair. "Cute," he says, twirling the stem between his fingers.

Oy, I forgot Matan filled my hair with white, purple, and yellow wildflowers. I must look like a clown.

"Your father wanted me to tell you everyone's at my house eating what you call lunch. If you want to join them, follow me."

I step beside him as he's walking, but then I stop. "Why didn't he tell me himself?"

Avi shoots me a withering glance. "He also wanted me to apologize for watching you undress the first night you were here."

"Well?"

"Israelis don't apologize for what they're not sorry for."

Now I'm really getting riled up. "You're *not* going to apologize?"

He looks at me straight in the eye. "What I saw was beautiful and natural, so why should I say sorry?"

12

Boys are either jerks or clueless.
Take your pick.

"Ron, I need to call home and my cell phone won't work."

I've been in Israel almost six weeks and need to call home once again. First of all, Mitch is back from his camping trip and I need to talk to him. Second of all, I need to call Mom and Jessica.

Ron is sitting on the couch watching some news channel in Hebrew. Uncle Chime is with him, along with the corkscrew-haired Matan.

Matan is naked and he's been like that for the better part of my trip so far. Who am I to bring it up to them that their son isn't dressed and his pee-wee is dangling out for all the *moshav* to see. You'd think they would have noticed they're not living in a nudist colony.

"I think your mom was going out of town," Ron says, his face still turned toward the television.

"So I'll call a friend."

"What's the number," he says as he heads toward the phone in the kitchen.

Obviously, like everywhere else around here, there's no privacy.

I recite Mitch's number and then he hands me the phone. I pull up a chair in front of the refrigerator and park myself there for the call.

"Hello," a scratchy voice answers.

"Mitch?" I say.

"Yeah?"

"It's Amy."

"Huh?"

"You know, your girlfriend," I say, starting to get pissed.

"Hey, babe. Sorry I haven't called, I got back late last night. Do you know what time it is?" he says, his voice still ragged.

"I'm in Israel, Mitch. And no, I don't know what time it is in Chicago because *I'm halfway across the globe.*"

"Wait, you lost me. Israel?"

"Are you sleeping or listening to me? 'Cause I can only make one call here and I've chosen to call you. It's like jail."

I hear him yawn and I can tell he's attempting to sit up instead of lie in bed. Hopefully now he'll pay some attention to what I'm saying.

"Mitch?"

"Wait, I gotta pee."

I have an urge to bang my head against the wall.

"Can't it wait?"

"No."

I'm trying to disguise my annoyance in front of the rest of the family.

"Well, can you hurry it up a bit? This is long distance, you know."

"I'm tryin', babe."

In the background I hear a stream of pee hitting water and Mitch lets out a long, satisfying sigh. I don't know if I should feel flattered he feels comfortable enough to pee while he's on the phone with me, or grossed out.

"You done?" I ask after I hear a loud flush.

"Yeah," he says. "I'm back in my room."

"You didn't wash your hands."

I mean, if I heard him pee and flush I would have definitely heard the sound of him washing his hands.

"You just told me to hurry up. If I wash my hands I have to put the phone down. You wanna wait?"

"I guess not. Just remember to wash them when you get off with me," I say. "And then disinfect the phone with antibacterial spray."

"Leave it to you, Amy, to tell it like it is."

Unfortunately, Snotty opens the front door and walks in the house with Ofra. Avi, Doo-Doo, and Moron follow them into the house. Great. Just my luck. Now I have a bigger audience to eavesdrop on my conversation with my boyfriend.

Out of the corner of my eye I catch Avi looking at me, his jaw tense. I haven't talked to him since he *purposely* didn't apologize for watching me undress. I think we've been avoiding each other, actually. Which is just fine with me.

I turn my chair around so I'm facing the wall and say quietly into the phone, "You know what I like about you?"

"Shit," Mitch says, "I just stubbed my toe on my skateboard."

It's not the response I was aiming for.

"You okay?" I ask, trying not to lose my patience.

"I think I'm bleeding. Wait a minute."

As I wonder how much a phone call costs per minute from Israel to the United States, I twirl the cord around my finger.

It's hard while I'm waiting not to turn around to catch a glimpse of what the others are doing. They're talking loudly in Hebrew.

I can't stand it anymore. I take a glimpse at Avi. He's wearing a black T-shirt with some Hebrew lettering on it and faded jeans ripped in both knees. He's also wearing a silver-linked chain around his wrist.

Now, I've seen boys wear jewelry before and haven't thought it enhances masculinity in the least. But Avi wears the bracelet like it's a manly accessory. He makes the other guys look dorky for not having a silver link chain bracelet on their wrists.

When my gaze travels up, I feel like a Peeping Tom when I realize he's caught me checking him out. Lifting the bracelet hand, he gives me a mock salute.

I can feel my face turn red and my blood starts to pound loudly in my head. He's seen me check him out. I want to die now, especially when he then walks up to Snotty and grabs her hand. That hand holding Snotty's is the same one that held my snake-guts-covered foot two weeks ago.

"Okay, I'm back," Mitch says. "No blood, but it still hurts like a bitch."

I forgot I was even on hold and, to be honest, wasn't paying attention to what Mitch just said. Turning back around, I giggle softly into the phone. Avi is trying to concentrate on Snotty, but I know for a fact he's listening to my end of the conversation.

"What's so funny?" Mitch asks. "I'm hurting here and all you can do is laugh?"

Have you ever tried to make other people think you're having a good time when you're not? What sucks is when the person you're with doesn't get it. They need to play along, but you can't tell them for fear of being discovered. *Play along with me, Mitch.*

"I can't wait to go camping with you," I say.

Let Snotty and all of them realize I have someone back home waiting for me. For some reason I'll feel like less of a loser here for hanging out by myself every day.

"What's wrong with you?" he says. "You hate camping."

"Of course I do," I say, then giggle again.

Giggling doesn't come naturally to me, but I do a pretty good job of making it sound authentic. I think.

Although my boyfriend now thinks I'm a freakoid.

"What about our tickets to the BoDeans concert at Ravinia for next weekend?" he says. "I spent fourteen bucks on those tickets, along with the extra thirty I spent on the Renaissance Faire tickets. You said you'd go with me."

Thankfully, the group heads outside. I let out a breath because I can finally be myself again.

I turn back around in the chair and stare at a flying spider-like thingy near the ceiling.

"Yeah, well that was before I got sucked into going to a country infested with Ferragamo-stealing mutts and flying spiders."

"Huh?"

"Forget it. I wish I could be there with you, really I do."

God, I hope he doesn't ask Roxanne Jeffries to go out with him. She's his next-door neighbor and has been flirting with him all year. He even told me she undresses with the curtains wide open.

"Say, I've got an awesome idea. Take Jessica. She's not doing anything this summer except working at a day camp for kids. She'll go with you." And she'll keep an eye on you for me.

"Don't you think it'd be weird if I go out with your best friend?"

"It's not like it'd be romantic or anything."

Jessica doesn't even think Mitch is cute. She's told me he reminds her of a poodle on Prozac. Everyone's entitled to an opinion. Mom always says, "Opinions are like assholes, everybody's got one and everyone thinks everyone else's stinks." It's true.

90

"I guess I could call her," he finally says.

"Tell her I miss her."

"Sure. When are you coming back?"

If I can manipulate Ron, very soon. "Before school starts, but who knows." We both go to Chicago Academy, a private high school.

He yawns. "Have fun."

As if. "You, too. Don't miss me too much."

He gives a short laugh before saying, "Bye, Amy."

I think I hear the phone click before I answer, "Bye."

13

A star is just a star.
Or is it?

It's nine o'clock the next morning and I'm bored, as usual.
I eat breakfast, alone again, as I watch *Safta* sit in her chair.
Snotty came home late last night, her friends all laughing
and making noise at two o'clock in the morning. I hate to
admit it, but I'm sorry I stayed home. With the exception
of Snotty and Avi, hanging with the group is kind of fun.

"Your *aba* wants you to go to the *sheeps*. He's waiting
for you," *Safta* says.

"I don't want to."

I know I sound like a little kid, but why go into detail
and hurt the ol' woman.

"He misses you."

What? He wouldn't miss me even if I disappeared from this earth.

"I don't think so," I say as I stuff hummus into a pita and take a bite.

"He loves his homeland and wants to share it with you."

I have a mouth full of hummus as I blurt out, "Why doesn't he move back here if he loves it so much?"

"I bet you know the answer to that question, Amy. He stays away because of you. You're his family. His future. His blood. Wherever you are is his home now."

I kneel beside her while I listen to her voice. It's soothing, and when she talks it almost sounds like a lullaby. I'm loud. My mom is loud. I talk loud. I walk loud. I'm just a loud person. But this old lady is like cotton, everything about her is soft and quiet. She leans over and takes something out of her pocket.

"Hold out your hand," she says.

I hold my hand out. She drops something into it and gently closes my fingers over my palm.

"What is it?" I ask.

"Look at it."

I open my fist and look at a small gold and diamond Jewish star glittering in the center of my palm. It's attached to a thin gold necklace. The star is smaller than a nickel, just big enough to know what it is, but small enough to be almost . . . private.

I don't know what to say to her. Being Jewish isn't a part of me. Mom doesn't believe in religion so I've never been to church except for my cousin's wedding. I've never been to a synagogue, either, except for Jessica's bat mitzvah.

"I'd like you to have it," *Safta* says. "It's called the *Magen David*, the star of David."

Man, I want it. I don't know why I want it, but I do. I'm not Jewish and would feel like a huge faker if I did take it. I mean, I could never wear it or anything. It's just so shiny and glittery and it actually means something important to *Safta*.

"I can't take this," I say. When I note the disappointment in the eyes that are an exact replica of mine I add, "It's too beautiful."

"You have something else to say, don't you?"

How does she know?

I stand up and say, "I'm not Jewish."

I can't look at her. If I do, I might see she's upset because a non-Jewish girl is her granddaughter. I don't know how Israelis feel about non-Jews. For some reason I don't want to know if she resents me. 'Cause I like *Safta*. A lot.

"Look at me, my sweet Amy."

Me? Sweet? I raise my eyes and look straight at her.

She's smiling, the wrinkles around her eyes making deep creases as she takes my hand in hers, the one still holding the necklace with the small Jewish star pendant.

"Being Jewish is more in your heart than in your mind. For some, being Jewish is strictly following the laws and customs of our ancestors. For others, it's being part of a community. Religion is very personal. It will always be there for you if you want or need it. You can choose to embrace it or decide your life doesn't need it. Nobody can force religion on you or it's not real."

Looking down at the necklace in my hand, I say, "Can I keep it? Just for a little while. I'll give it back, I promise."

She pats the top of my head. "I used to wonder why my son stayed away from Israel for so long, but I see the way he looks at you. He wants to protect you, keep you from hurt or harm while trying to respect that inner fire you possess. It is genuine and pure. Take the necklace," she says, then hesitates before adding, "for as long as you want it."

Staring at this woman, who has eyes that mirror mine and who says words that turn my world upside down, disturbs my inner being. I clutch the necklace in my hand. Then I turn around and head for the refrigerator, looking for some water. Even though it's right in front of my face as I open the door, my limbs feel paralyzed.

I close the fridge and turn to *Safta* as I walk toward the door.

"I think I'll take a walk," I say.

I take one more look at the necklace before gently placing it in my back pocket.

I find myself walking toward the sheep. When I get close to the pens, the Ferragamo-stealing mutt bounds toward me. Its filthy tail is wagging furiously, fanning his behind. Remembering my toes filled with snake-guts, I walk right past the dog and ignore its pathetic attempts at making up with me.

"Arg!"

I look down at the thing. "Arg, yourself. Where's my sandal?"

"Arg!" Wag. "Arg!" Wag.

He trots off toward a hilly area beyond the pens and I think of how lucky that dog is to be free to do as he pleases. Even steal other people's shoes without repercussions.

I walk farther into the pens, the sound of baying sheep and electric razors leading me in the right direction. Spotting Ron, I head toward him. I convince myself that as long as I just hang out here, there's no reason Ron will think I'm incompetent and regret I'm his daughter.

"Amy, honey, over here!"

My eyes wander to the direction of Ron's voice. He's never called me honey before and it kind of startles me. What does that mean, anyway? Honey. It's sweet, but it's also sticky and doesn't come off your hands easily. Annoyingly sweet. Is that me? Not on your life.

He's leaning down, and his knees are locking a sheep down while he's shearing its wooly hair off. The sheep doesn't seem to mind, but I do.

"Ron, that's inhumane," I say.

He finishes running the razor through the sheep's fur while the fluff falls beside him. He finally releases the poor, naked animal and looks up at me.

"You have a better way?" he asks.

It's then I realize Ron isn't the only one shearing the sheep. O'dead is next to Ron, Doo-Doo is next to O'dead, Uncle Chime is next to Doo-Doo, and Avi is next to my uncle. They're all exhausted, I can tell by the way they're breathing heavily and their shirts are wet with sweat. Not just their armpits and chests, their entire shirts are soaked through.

And they're all staring at me. Except O'dead. He's staring at Snotty, across in another pen. Hmmm.

The razor sounds stop and I feel like the world has, too. I think of something quick to say.

It comes to me like lightning and I blurt out, "Why don't you just leave the fur on?" Duh. It sounds so simple I give a short laugh.

Chuckles from my right side alert me to my cousin and Ofra. Snotty's wearing a tight black shirt and her dark makeup is running down her cheeks while feeding a lamb with a bottle. Hasn't she ever heard of waterproof mascara? Or the term *less is more?*

"They'll be too hot during summer months," Ron explains.

I sit down on one of the metal railings and watch. There are dogs in the middle of the pens, eating something red and gooey on the ground. My lips curl.

"What are the dogs eating?" I ask. Maybe I don't want to know, but my curiosity gets the best of me.

"One of the female sheep had a baby this morning."

"They're eating a lamb?"

"No, the placenta. It's very nutritious."

I gag. "Eww!" I say.

I shouldn't have asked. If I hadn't asked, I wouldn't know. GROSS! Baby sheep placenta. Blech! Stop thinking about it. Stop thinking about it.

But the more I will myself to stop thinking about it the more I can't look away. Kind of like those bloody crime scenes they show on television. You don't want to watch, but can't help it.

Out of the corner of my eye I see Mutt coming into the enclosure. He's small enough to go under the metal railings. When he looks at me, I squint at him.

"Do NOT eat sheep placenta," I tell him.

He nods at me, as if he understands what I just said. Then he tromps over to the placenta, starts to lick it, takes a part of the gooey, bloody thing in his mouth and tugs at it. I can't look any more.

If only Jessica were here, we could have a huge laugh at the whole grody situation. But she's not.

I walk over to where the newborn sheep are. A baby lamb stumbles over to me and I pet it with my hand.

"Hey sweetheart," I say.

"Baa," it whines back, which makes me smile.

I think it's the first time I've smiled since Matan put the flowers in my hair.

"Don't get too attached, he's going to be killed soon."

My heart sinks and my smile fades as quickly as it appeared. I turn to Snotty while I pick up the baby lamb.

"What?" I say.

"We have them slaughtered at three months old. That one's a boy so he'll be one of the first to go."

I look into the eyes of the small, helpless newborn and pull it closer to me protectively.

I'm a carnivore. Although meeting the animal I'm going to eat up close and personal makes me sick to my stomach. He's so cute. How can I even think about the poor guy being slaughtered? Maybe I won't cut out carbs after all.

Matan comes trotting up the lane with *Doda* Yucky behind him. He's naked, as usual. What's funny is I'm getting so used to seeing the kid naked that it doesn't even faze me.

He comes into the pen and runs around with the lambs. He's screeching in delight as he runs and tries to catch them.

After a minute the lambs start running after him. But it's not to play, I realize they think his little pee-wee is another baby bottle nipple. He's laughing and running away from the lambs that are trying to get milk out of his thingy like it's a game. Looking around, I notice *Doda* Yucky is laughing, as well as the rest of the people who have now stopped shearing the sheep.

I run over to Matan and pick his naked little body up to protect him from the perverted lambs.

After I carry him back to safety, I say very loudly to anyone who can hear me, "That. Is. *Not*. Okay."

Matan isn't fazed, neither is anyone else. They're still laughing. *Doda* Yucky talks to Uncle Chime before she and Matan trot happily back to the house, thank goodness.

The razors start up again, all the men except for Ron bending over the poor sheep. He says something to Uncle Chime in Hebrew before coming over to me.

"I have a job for you," he says.

14

Determination and skill is half of
the job. Dumb luck is the other half.

I follow him to the other end of the enclosure, which is thankfully in the shade.

"When the *sheeps* are done being sheared, herd them into this pen."

I look over at the skinny, bare-assed animal. Man, they looked so fat, puffy, and large with all that fuzzy hair, it's unbelievable how much smaller and vulnerable they look after a shave. I can just sense their self-consciousness as a shiver runs through my bones.

But I'm determined to help. I think. *Don't screw this up, Amy.* My eyes wander to Snotty, feeding the baby animals with bottles of milk. That looks like fun. Why do I get stuck with herding the bare-assed ones into a pen?

What if they start getting frisky with me? Worse, what if they start getting frisky with each other? Blech!

"You able to do it?" Ron asks.

"Of course," I say with more conviction than I feel. "Piece of cake," I add.

If I do this, maybe he'll be proud of me.

Uncle Chime lets one of the sheep go and it struggles to its feet. It's a male one, I can tell by the dangling thing in between its legs. And he's staring at me from the corner of the pen.

"Go on," I say.

But above the buzzing of the shearing I bet he can't hear me.

The sheep stares at me with his big, spooky, gray eyes. I wonder if he'll charge me. I move a step closer. He doesn't move.

"Go on," I say a bit louder this time.

Sincerely hoping nobody is watching me, I take another step toward the animal.

He backs up.

"This way, dummy," I say.

The thing won't listen to me. Damn. I look over at Ron, but thankfully he's not paying attention.

It's me against the sheep. Did I say the thing looked small and vulnerable after being shaved? I take that back. Before I step toward the menacing four-legged, bare-assed sheep with a dangling thing between its legs, out of the corner of my eye I see another sheep stand up. It heads next to the first one. Now I have two to deal with.

Avi stands up and heads over to get another fuzzy, fur-filled sheep to shear. As he does, our eyes meet. I still haven't forgiven him for the snake-guts incident. It's unbelievable he won't apologize for watching me while I was as naked as the sheep he's shearing. Kind of ironic, isn't it? I plead to him with my eyes, *Help me*.

He looks back at me with contempt. *Not on your life, Amy. You're on your own*. Jerk. Not that he actually voiced those words, but I know he was thinking it.

Screw him. I take another step toward the two sheep. Maybe if I channel their psyche they'll do what I want. I open my eyes wide and look at the bigger one intently. *Go inside the pen*, I urge with my mind. Focus, Amy, I tell myself. I put my fingertips on my temples in order to channel my thoughts to the damn four-legged creature who's looking at me like I'm a nutcase.

I feel a presence standing beside me. Turning abruptly, I almost knock into Avi. The confused expression on his face, with furrowed eyebrows and chocolate irises, tells me he thinks I'm a mashed potato (which, just in case you aren't familiar with the slang term, means a brainless human being).

"Yah!" he yells while stomping his foot on the ground. This coming from a guy who thinks *I'm* a mashed potato.

I turn back to the sheep, who have now just run into the adjacent pen at his command/stomp routine.

Avi's got this arrogant smirk on his face like he's done some massive accomplishment.

"I bet your boyfriend can't do that," he says.

How dare he bring Mitch into this . . . this . . . this . . . "I bet he wouldn't even want to," I say back.

For the rest of the afternoon, I copy the yell-stomp technique Avi showed me and I've become quite the herder.

At one point Ron even said, "Good job, honey." He'll never know how much those words meant to me.

Right after the adults leave the pens for the day, I watch as the teens gather together on bales of hay over ten feet tall.

I walk past them until Ofra yells down at me. "Amy, come up here."

Snotty glares at her, but Ofra ignores her.

"No, thanks," I say.

Avi is up there, sitting like he was born ten feet off the ground.

"She's scared to climb up here," he says. "She's got big words, but little courage."

Unbelievable. One minute he's trying to help me and the next he's being the biggest showoff and insulting me. It doesn't take more to get me climbing up the yellow, wiry straw.

When I get to the top, I don't know where to sit. I hang my feet over the edge of the hay and lean back. All eyes are on me. I turn to Avi and give him a little to stew about.

"Why do you hate me?" I ask.

I know this shouldn't be laundered in public like this, but I can't help it. I need to know, and I need to know now.

Avi doesn't answer and everyone else is looking away from him.

"Don't take it personally," Doo-Doo says. "He's been like this for a while."

"Why?" I direct my question to Doo-Doo, but I'm still looking at Avi.

Nobody says anything. The tension is as hot as the sun beating down on my back.

Avi barks out words in Hebrew I obviously can't possibly understand. My Hebrew vocabulary is limited to about five words. He knows this. Snotty knows this. Hell, they all know it.

Which makes me feel like one of those flying spider-looking things back at the house. Not a spider, not a fly. Just somewhere in-between.

They all start arguing. At once. Very loudly. It sounds like one big phlegm-fest because it seems as if every word in Hebrew has the 'ch' sound coming out of the middle of their throats.

It'd be nice to know what they're all talking about. Are they discussing why Avi hates me? It sure feels that way. But they're arguing.

It's obvious Avi and Snotty hate me, I'm so glad the other kids have been nice. O'dead leans his body closer to Snotty's each time he talks. Interesting observation I'll reserve for later. I wonder what it is about her that attracts all the guys? Anyone can have black makeup running down their face.

I stand, ready to climb down from this haystack. I feel so uncomfortable around Avi and Snotty.

"You want to come on a camping trip with us?" Doo-Doo asks.

My eyebrows furrow. Before I can answer, Avi interrupts me.

"*Mah-pee-tome!*" Avi says to Doo-Doo.

"*Llama-low?*" Doo-Doo says back to his friend.

"Hello? Why don't you speak English?" I finally say. "Don't you realize it's rude to talk privately while I'm right in front of you?"

Ofra leans back on her elbows and nods her head. "She has a point."

My eyes blink. I could almost kiss the girl on the lips for supporting me so much. Although I don't go that way. But if I did, I would.

Avi groans.

"I don't go camping," I say.

"You said you were going with your boyfriend. I heard you on the phone," Avi challenges.

Think quick, Amy. He's got your number.

"Yeah, well, I only go with him. Mitch has been a Boy Scout since he was, like, five years old or something."

Snotty hisses. "Amy, you make up stuff to try and look good. What's real with you and what's not? Avi's right about you."

Silence. Until I feel my patience snap inside my body.

I know I shouldn't start up with someone I have to share a room with. And I know it probably isn't the smartest thing to go off on my cousin in front of an audience. She probably won't understand what I'm going to say anyway because of the language barrier. But I can't help it, there's like an overload of adrenaline running through my brain.

Even as I tell myself to keep my mouth closed, I hear myself say, "Do you get off on being a royal bitch? 'Cause ever since I met you, you've treated me like a piece of shit." I'm on a roll and my mouth is working overtime. "I can't stand you, your short shirts, tight pants . . . or your sorry excuse for breasts! How's that for being real?"

I wave my finger at Avi. "And you, all you've got to offer is a bad attitude and a chip on your shoulder. I *will* go camping, just to piss . . . you . . . off! You don't like it, don't go. Then you can be an Israeli with a big mouth and little courage."

"You think you got courage?" Avi challenges me.

"Damn straight. I could push you off this thing without thinking twice."

He stands up, his mouth upturned in a smirk. "I dare you."

Okay, I think about it. But only once. Then I push his chest with all the strength I have.

He doesn't budge, the guy is like a rock.

When I hear his laugh, I turn around and jump down the piles of hay until I reach the ground. Wouldn't you know it a feeling of rationality comes over me right now. And I think:

I don't know why tears are rolling down my face.

I don't know why I just blew up at two people I'm going to have to see for the next month.

And I sure as hell don't know why I agreed to go on a camping trip in the middle of a war zone with people who hate me.

God, I'm in Israel, the Holy Land. Where are you?

15

When the pickins are slim,
you take what you can get.

That night after dinner, I'm watching television with *Doda*
Yucky when Snotty's friends come barging in the door.
Why don't people lock their doors around here?

Snotty and Ofra come out of the bedroom dressed
in slinky, short, tight-fitting dresses. Avi, Doo-Doo, and
O'dead are wearing jeans with long-sleeve T-shirts.

I don't ask where they're going tonight, because I don't
care. I'm perfectly happy to sit in front of the television all
day. I've been pleasantly surprised that there's a lot of American shows on TV in Israel. That's probably why Israelis
know so much English.

Ron, who has been talking on the phone most of the
evening, comes over to me. "The kids are going to a disco."

A disco? Discos went out in, like, the seventies. "Good for them," I say.

"Don't you want to go?"

"No."

"It might be fun to get off the *moshav*."

If he only knew what I said to O'snot earlier. I insulted her clothes *and* her boobs. I'm not about to admit those little facts to Ron.

"I'm going to ask them to take you," he says, and before I can stop him he stands up and walks over to Snotty. He says something in Hebrew to her.

She says something back.

At this point *Doda* Yucky interrupts her, her voice in a scolding tone. Then my aunt walks over to me and takes my hand. "O'snot wants to take you out with her friends."

Yeah, right. But the lady just fought on my behalf, and I don't have the heart to argue with her. Instead, I shoot a scalding look at Ron, the person who got me into this mess in the first place.

Ten minutes later I find myself in Avi's car, being driven down the mountain. Avi and Snotty ignore me, but I don't blame them. I hate them, they hate me. It's a mutual hate-hate relationship.

When we pull up to the "disco," I get out of the car and follow Snotty, Ofra, Doo-Doo, O'dead, and Avi to the entrance. It looks like a large warehouse. Loud music is blaring from the place and colorful, blinking lights are shining through large windows.

I halt as soon as I scan the long line of people waiting to get in. "Is it safe?" I ask.

"I promise there aren't any snakes inside for you to accidentally step on," Snotty says, then laughs at me.

My eyes flash in outrage as I focus on Avi. How could he have told Snotty about the snake-guts mishap? What a betrayal. Now I feel humiliated because of him.

"Come on," Ofra says, locking my arm with hers as she leads me to the line.

I toss my hair back and stand in line. When I reach the front, an army guard makes me open my purse and he checks the contents. I expect him to ask me for an ID, but he doesn't. I guess in Israel there are no age restrictions for dance clubs. When the army guy waves me on, I have to go through a metal detector in order to enter the 'disco.'

Boy, they're not taking any chances. If we had a soldier at the entrance to every town, shopping mall, and bar in the United States, we'd be out of soldiers. There wouldn't be anyone left to protect our country.

I walk in, and the floor is vibrating to the beat of the music because it's so loud. Snotty, Ofra, O'dead, and Doo-Doo go directly to the dance floor and start dancing. Avi is leaning against a railing, brooding as usual. But he's surrounded by girls while he's standing there so he doesn't look like a loner.

Me? Well, I'm standing here alone because I don't feel like dancing right now. It's wall-to-wall people, but I manage to squeeze through the crowd, heading for the bar. I need a Coke, or at least something in my hand so I'm not just standing around staring at people.

Luckily, I snag the only open barstool before anyone else can get their butt on it.

I take a moment to take it all in. The people at the disco are wearing very trendy outfits. They're also dancing, laughing, and drinking. The air smells like cigarette smoke; obviously there aren't smoking laws here.

I don't go to clubs back home because I'm only sixteen and they won't let me in until I'm twenty-one. But when I do, I'm going to have as much fun as these Israelis.

The bartender says something to me in Hebrew and places a beer mug in front of me with yellow liquid inside.

"I speak English," I say at the top of my lungs so he can hear me above the music.

He leans forward and says in my ear, "The guy over there bought you the drink."

He points to the other end of the bar, where a guy wearing a white button-down shirt with most of the buttons undone is sitting. Is he kidding? The guy looks as if he's about Avi's age, and has long hair. And it's not cool long hair, it looks like it's been greased back with too much hair gel. He's probably the *one* uncool guy in the whole place.

Great. I'm an uncool guy magnet.

To my horror, the guy is walking over to me as if he's some macho dude. He's wearing a huge grin on his face, which looks like it hasn't been shaved in a week.

I need help here.

Snotty and the gang are on the dance floor so they won't be much help. I search the room for Avi, who's obviously moved away from the railing. If I find him, I could pretend he's my date so this guy will leave me alone.

When my eyes finally settle on Avi, I realize he's not brooding anymore. He's dancing with some Hilary Duff look-alike.

To make matters worse, he's a good dancer. Not one of those guys who only moves from side to side. No, Avi moves like he's been born to dance with a girl in his arms.

I watch in disgust as he leans forward and says something into her ear, then they both laugh. For some reason I wish it wasn't so loud that he would have to be so close to her to talk. I don't care about him, I'm just pissed that he's having a good time and I'm not.

"*Allo, ay zeh cusit,*" Uncool Guy says once he's weaved his way through the crowd and is now standing in front of me.

"I speak English," I say, shrugging apologetically.

"My English not so good," he says. "You American?"

"Yes."

His eyes light up. "You want dance with me? My dancing better than my English."

I peer around him and take a peek at Avi, who is still dancing with his blond bimbo. Grabbing the guy's hand, I lead him to the middle of the dance floor.

I've taken classes at Julie's Dance Studio since I was four years old, so I'm not afraid to let loose. Listen, I wouldn't choose this guy to dance with, but at this point I can't be picky.

As I listen to the music, I pretend I'm dancing with my boyfriend. When the guy puts his hands around my waist, I want to think it's Mitch's hands holding me against him.

I close my eyes. The only problem is that in my imagination they're not Mitch's hands. They're Avi's. The guy I hate is haunting pure thoughts of me and my boyfriend.

Wait a minute. I think the guy I'm dancing with is feeling my back as if he's trying to locate the clasp on my bra. I open my eyes and whip around to face the *perv*. Lucky for me my bra fastens in the front.

I stop dancing. The perv leans forward to talk to me— it's too loud to hear unless the person is screaming in your ear. I think he's about to apologize, until I feel this slimy wet thing trying to climb into my ear canal.

What the hell *is* that?

When I realize Uncool Guy is trying to turn me on by sliding his Gene Simmons tongue around my ear and trying to shove it down my ear canal, I shriek and push him back. Anything to get his tongue as far away from my ear as possible.

Unfortunately, I've pushed him into some other people who were dancing. They're not too happy with me or the licker and push him back. This starts more pushing, and soon the place is out of control.

Oh, crap.

I'm lost in the crowd, unable to move because the crowd has turned into a mob. When someone grabs my hand and leads me out, I'm grateful.

Until I recognize Avi's bracelet attached to that hand.

I stumble outside with Avi and the rest of the mob. They've cleared out the club. When I see a police car with its lights flashing, I panic. Because someone over by the police car is talking to the soldiers and policemen while pointing at me.

"Shit. Amy, don't say anything," Avi says. "Let me talk."

When the soldiers and policeman come up to us, I zip my mouth shut.

"*Mah aseet*," the soldier says.

When Avi starts to talk, the guy puts up a hand and points to me.

I wanted to keep my mouth shut, I really did. My intentions were to stand here and stay silent. "I speak English," I blurt out.

"Did you start pushing people on the dance floor?" the soldier guy asks gruffly.

"Only because of the ear licker. I mean, at first he tried to feel me up but then, well, I thought he was going to apologize. Instead, my ear starts getting slimy and I realize he's not apologizing, he's giving my ear a tongue bath."

I know I'm rambling. I'm scared, and I know I deserve to be punished for causing a whole club to clear out because of me. A cold knot is forming in my stomach and I clutch Avi's hand.

Then, suddenly, out of the corner of my eye I catch a glimpse of the guy with the tongue. "There he is!" I yell.

The licker just backs up and disappears behind a car.

The soldier barks out orders at Avi and storms off.

"What did he say?"

"To take you home now or else he'll arrest you. Come on," he says.

"Do you have a Q-tip?" I ask him.

"Why?"

Duh! "So I can wipe that guy's germs out of my ear. I bet I already have an ear infection because of that dude."

He's walking so fast I can hardly keep up with him.

"You don't blame me for what happened back there, do you?"

When we reach Avi's car, he turns to me. "You were turning that guy on with your dancing. What did you expect?"

I meet his accusing eyes without flinching. "He knew I was American. Maybe Israelis like wet tongues in their ear, but in America—"

"He knew you were American?"

"Yeah. I told him when he bought me the beer."

"Beer? You were drinking alcohol with that guy? No wonder he thought you were easy."

"For your information, I am not easy."

"American girls have a reputation around here."

"Stop using me as proof of your stereotypes, Avi. It's not fair. Besides, you were shakin' it plenty tonight. You're just jealous because your blond bimbo didn't want to suck *your* ear off."

Snotty and friends are walking toward us. I cross my arms in front of my chest, waiting for them so we can go home.

"Someone started a fight inside the disco," Ofra says to me, offering her explanation of the commotion.

I bite my tongue and keep silent, but Avi glances sideways at me.

"You," Snotty says. "You started it, didn't you? I should have guessed. You can't do anything right."

"Leave her alone," Doo-Doo says. I want to kiss him right now for sticking up for me.

Feeling like I have support, I say to Snotty defiantly, "I can do anything you can do." And then, because adrenaline is flowing through my body I add, "And I can do it better."

The look on her face is priceless. She's thinking. I can almost hear her rusty, unused brain creaking as it's working. "Shear a sheep," she blurts out. "Tomorrow morning."

"No problem," I say with confidence, even though on the inside I'm shuddering at the thought of holding down a poor, defenseless sheep while I cut his fur off until he's naked.

But I'll do it, just to prove to everyone I don't screw everything up.

I just hope I don't make a fool out of myself.

16

I can do anything you can do,
and I can do it better. I think.

Just call me Amy the Sheep Shearer. That's what I've been
trying to convince myself of all morning. After I found the
note that Snotty wants to meet me after breakfast for our
little challenge, that is.

Unfortunately, last night was not a nightmare. I really
and truly challenged Snotty, and I hadn't even had any of
that beer I was accused of consuming. Okay, I realize I'm
the stupid one here, but I'm still determined to prove to
her that I do not screw everything up.

I dress in jeans and a long-sleeve T-shirt for full protec-
tion. I don't have any protective goggles, so I put on my
Coach sunglasses. Walking outside, I see Mutt bouncing
toward me.

"You find my sandal yet?"

To answer me, he rolls onto his back. His tongue is hanging out of his mouth like a beggar.

"Don't grovel," I say. "It's not attractive."

I pick the mutt up and carry him with me. He might prove useful when I'm trying to corner the sheep. "Okay," I say. "Let's get a game plan. You make me look good, and I'll forget the sandal incident. Okay?"

Mutt's answer is a big fart.

This is not going to be my day.

When I reach the sheep pens, Ofra is the first person I see.

"You don't have to do this," she says.

Oh, yes I do. For me. For Mutt. For Americans all over the globe. Ofra's lack of confidence in me just furthers my resolve.

"That's okay. I want to do it," I assure her.

Doo-Doo comes over to me and gives me pointers. "Hold him down. Keep your eye on him. Don't drop the razor on your toe."

He's like a boxing coach, and in the ring is my opponent.

They've placed one sheep in the pen, along with a large razor hanging from the ceiling. Doo-Doo helps me strap the razor to my hand.

I survey my surroundings. Snotty is sitting on top of a railing with O'dead at her side. Ofra and Doo-Doo, my supporters, are beside me.

Avi is nowhere in sight. I'm surprised he didn't come to watch me get eaten alive by a sheep.

In the opposite pen is another sheep. Snotty's. I swear, it looks a lot smaller than mine.

Taking a deep breath, I enter the pen with the unsuspecting animal. He's even bigger than I thought. You'd think Snotty would have enough compassion to give me a lamb like the one in the nursery rhyme, but no.

This is definitely not Mary's little lamb. And its fleece is as dirty as Mutt's, not white as snow.

Snotty enters the other pen. She jumps right in, like she does this every day. Then she turns to me. "You're really going to go through with it?"

"Hell, yeah." I once saw a bumper sticker that showed a picture of an American flag and the caption below *These Colors Don't Run*. I'm not about to chicken out. Even though I really, really want to.

"Okay," she says, pure disbelief on her face. "On the count of three we'll start. Whoever finishes first, wins."

"Fair enough."

"One. Two. Three."

I put Mutt down and whisper, "Go do your thing."

Immediately, Mutt starts barking and the sheep scurries into the corner. I turn on the razor and head toward the menacing animal.

Until it looks at me with those big, gray eyes. I keep thinking that Ron told me it's too hot for them with their hair all bushy. I understand and sympathize. Okay, I'm trying to convince myself that I understand and sympathize.

It's not working.

I look down at Mutt, who's staring at me as if saying, *Do it!* He's right. There's no chickening out now. I have to face my fears and just do it. I hold up the razor like a sword and head into battle.

Except the stupid sheep runs away in fear. When it passes me, I hold out the razor like an idiot. Now the thing has a bald stripe down its back.

I try not to listen to or look at the progress in the other pen. I'm trying to concentrate solely on my mission. Mutt is barking up a storm, making the sheep nervous.

"Wrestle him to the ground and hold him there," I hear from my cheering section.

Should I break the news that I never had a brother to teach me to wrestle? Or a sister, for that matter.

"Mutt, you got to help me here."

Mutt is a great sheep herder. I realize this when the animal tries to move. Mutt expertly heads him off and gets him in the corner again.

With a swift move, I hold my weight against the wooly creature and start shearing. There's no rhyme or reason to it, I'm just so happy when the dirty, wooly fur starts flying off.

I hear lots of laughing, some cheering and various directions from Doo-Doo. I don't stop, I'm like a sheep shearing nut gone wild.

I step back and look at the poor animal. Okay, so I haven't done such a hot job. He has a Mohawk hairdo and his body looks like it's a road map. But I did it and I feel victorious.

Until I hear Ron's voice yell, "What the hell is going on here?"

17

This roller coaster called life
is making me dizzy.

"Amy, we need to talk."

I hate when parents think they can sit down and tell you what you've been doing wrong while they expect you to sit quiet and nod like a bobblehead figurine.

"What do you want?"

Right now I'm sitting outside the house petting Mutt. I'm proud of him, he's a great sheep herder. I can hear Uncle Chime yelling at Snotty inside the house. He didn't look too happy when Ron explained our little competition.

"I want to know what's going on with you," Ron says, sitting next to me.

"Nothing," I say.

He places one of his hands on my forearm. "Believe it or not, I want you to be happy. You don't have to shear sheep to prove anything to me."

I shrug his hand off me.

"If you want me to be happy, give me a ticket home right now. I don't belong here," I say. Then I add, "and I don't belong with you."

I don't know why I said it. I knew as the words left my lips it would hurt him. Maybe deep down I want to hurt him for not being there for me the past sixteen years of my life. I keep looking at Mutt and rubbing his tummy so I don't have to look at the disappointment of my life.

"Fine."

Wait. Did he just say "fine"? I think he did, but the word still doesn't register.

When I look up, Ron's back is to me. He's walking inside the house. My legs are a little numb from having the mutt on my lap for so long, but I scurry to get up and follow him.

When I enter the house, I walk up to him. He's rummaging through his suitcase.

"What did you say?" I ask.

He glances sideways at me before rummaging through his bag again. "I said 'fine,' Amy."

"Fine as in . . ."

"As in if you want me out of your life, if that will make you happy, then that's what I want for you." He takes papers out of his suitcase and holds them out to me. "Here's your ticket back to the States."

I hesitate for a moment. Then my hand reaches out and slips the paper out of his extended hand.

A wave of sorrow and confusion makes me freeze. Then I run out of the house and head to the place where *Safta* and I talked about her love for this place.

Sitting on the edge of the mountain, I think about everything here that I'll leave behind if I go home. Like Matan. Like my aunt and uncle, who I've just met. And Mutt.

But most of all, I want to be here for *Safta*. I love her, and can't just leave while I know she's going through chemo treatments.

I hug my knees to myself, thinking about this life here in Israel. It's a part of me, but not.

Walking back to the house, I look for Ron. I have to tell him I want to stay here for another reason, too: to find out where I fit into his life. When I see him talking on the phone, I sit on the kitchen chair, waiting.

Ron hands me the phone. "It's your mom. I called her."

"We need to talk, okay," I say to Ron before taking the phone out of his hand.

I watch as he nods, puts his hands in his pockets, and walks outside.

I put the receiver to my ear. "Hello?"

"Amy, are you okay? Ron just told me you want to come home."

"I did, but not anymore."

"You've changed your mind?"

"I guess," I say.

I hear her getting out of bed and closing a door. I bet she's locked herself in the bathroom because Marc with a "c" is in her bed and she doesn't want to wake the dork up.

After a minute she says to me in a very bubbly voice, "I have some great news."

"You broke up with Marc?" I say with a sigh of relief. "Finally."

"No, silly. Marc asked me to marry him last night. And I said yes."

"What!" I say as my heart sinks into my chest. This is not happening to me.

"It's so exciting," she says, oblivious to the fact that I'm totally freaking out here. "He had this special dinner planned. The ring was at the bottom of my champagne glass."

"He's a dork, Mom." Definitely NOT dad material. The ring at the bottom of the champagne glass is so cliché.

"He's one of the top real estate developers in the country. The new project on the Gold Coast, the most sought-after location in Chicago, is being done by his firm."

"So? We only have one parking spot for our condo. There's no room for his Mercedes," I say.

"I thought we'd look in the suburbs for a place. You know, something bigger . . . with a backyard and everything."

Huh? "As in you're moving to the 'burbs?"

"Isn't that wonderful!"

"Where does that leave me? Homeless?"

"Of course not, honey. Don't be ridiculous. Your home is with me and Marc."

Since when did "you and me" become "you, me, and Marc"?

Nice to know I'm important enough to consult with.

"Marc hates me, Mom." Right about now I feel as if everybody hates me.

"He does not. You haven't given him a fair chance."

I swallow hard and try not to cry.

"I know it's a shock to you, but I swear it's the best thing for us. We'll be a *family*."

I swear I'm going to hurl. A *family*? But Marc isn't my *family*.

"I thought you'd be happy. After you come back from Israel, you can help me plan for the wedding and look for a new house. We'll make a fresh start, the three of us."

I don't want a fresh start, I want an old start.

"I love you," she says.

If she loved me so much she would've thought before going ahead and screwing up my plans.

I have a huge lump in my throat when I say, "Congratulations. I love you, too."

"Bye, sweetheart. Call me next week, okay?" she says. "I just want us to be happy."

"Me, too," I say, then hang up. Happy is all in the eye of the beholder.

I march out of the house and spot Ron by an old, green tractor parked in the back of the house.

"You blew it!" I yell.

He has the audacity to look at me without saying anything.

I cross my arms in front of my chest. "Just keep standing there silent, Ron. You do that really well."

"What are you talking about?"

"I was just informed that Mom's dork boyfriend proposed to her. Couldn't *you* have proposed? It would have been nice to have my parents married; at the very least to say my parents were married at one point in time. But you were too selfish and worried about making sure you achieved the American Dream while basking in bachelorhood. You never fought for us. Worse, you never fought for me."

There, I finally said it. It may have taken me sixteen years and an attitude to cover up my insecurities, but I finally spilled the truth.

He blinks a couple of times, then says, "She's getting married?"

"I just said that, didn't I?"

He takes a deep breath, then sits on the bumper of the tractor. "Don't think I didn't fight, Amy. I asked her to marry me. And not just once. Before you were born and practically every time I saw her after your birth I got down on my knee. You were too busy running away from me to realize it."

"*If*, and I mean *if* you did propose, why didn't it happen? You were a commando, for God's sake. You're specially trained to get the mission accomplished."

He takes a long, deep breath. "She said she didn't want you growing up seeing a loveless marriage. She wanted to find a solid guy to be your *fadder*, not some Israeli immigrant. Every time I came to see you, I'd get a letter from her *fadder* threatening to tell the INS to cancel my visa. He accused me of getting her pregnant on purpose, to secure my American citizenship by marrying her. It wasn't true, but I feared never seeing you again. He was a powerful man, Amy."

He looks at me with a pained expression. "I don't expect you to understand."

"I do and I don't," I say, confused.

"When you told me to stop coming around, I didn't know what they'd told you about me. I just wanted a relationship with you, even if it was once a year."

"You're a real disappointment," I say.

I expect the you-must-respect-me-because-I'm-your-parent lecture, but instead Ron says, "You're right."

I'm shocked but say, "Damn straight I'm right. Maybe there's still a chance with Mom. You can call her and—"

"It's not going to change anything," he says, "and you know it. Deep down, you know she won't marry me."

"I feel so alone," I say, almost in a whisper.

"I love you," he says back. "It doesn't matter that you don't call me 'dad' or want to hug me. I've wanted that, but I want your friendship and trust even more."

This is a lot of information for me in one day. I need some time to digest it.

"I'm going to stay in Israel for the summer," I finally tell him. "Maybe we can, oh, I don't know."

The beginning of a smile tips the corners of his mouth.

With a shake of my head I say, "Don't get too excited, I'm still upset."

"I'm glad you're staying."

I turn around and head back into the house and into my bedroom.

Snotty is there.

Honestly, she's the last person I want to see. I remember I told her something about having small boobs or something like that, but it seems so long ago. I plop myself down on my bed.

"Are you packed?" she asks, bending over her backpack while putting things inside.

I lean back on my elbows. "For what?"

She turns around, those black-charcoal circles directed right at me. "Camping. You said you were going."

Laying back down on the bed, I say, "I lied."

"Just like an American."

"Excuse me? What's that supposed to mean?"

"Israelis say what we mean. You Americans just talk without meaning anything you say."

"We do not!" Geez, everyone is on my case lately. "For your information, I'm proud to be American. We may not always do or say the right thing, but what can you expect? Nobody wants to police the world, so they look to us to do it for them. We save everyone else's ass and then get blamed for it. Real fair, isn't it?"

Now I sound like an ambassador for the U.S.

Snotty lifts her backpack over her shoulder and walks out of the room.

"*Shalom*, Amy. We're leaving in ten minutes."

She leaves me with two choices: prove Snotty wrong and go on the camping trip to save face. Or stay on the moshav with nothing to do except herd bald sheep with Ron and Uncle Chime.

I walk into *Safta's* room and sit on the edge of her bed. My entire screwed-up life comes to a head and I'm completely confused.

"I need your advice."

She smiles warmly at me, like always. I am so happy to have her in my life, even if we did get a late start on getting to know each other.

"You see, it's like this," I say. I take a deep breath and let it all out as I talk. "My mom wants to marry her boyfriend, this guy I don't particularly like. Ron . . . you know, your son, has been a disappointment to me because to be honest he hasn't been a permanent fixture in my life. I resent them both, and I'm confused about who I am and where I fit in. And to top it off, O'snot is going on a trip with her friends, and I kind of want to get away and prove to her I'm capable, so I'm considering it."

Safta nods her head in thought, obviously understanding my predicament and giving it serious consideration.

"For a sixteen-year-old girl, you have a lot to deal with."

I let out another long breath. "Ain't that the truth."

"Maybe you need some time away. I think the camping trip is a good idea. Israel is a magical place, Amy. You just might find what you're looking for."

She's right. I need to get away from reality for a while. I kiss *Safta* on her cheek and head out of the room. But I stop at the door, turn around, and say, "I'm glad you're my *Safta*."

She tilts her head and smiles. "Me, too."

18

*Did you ever get the feeling you
were outnumbered?*

My heart is racing as I spot an empty backpack on the foot
of my bed. I must not have noticed it was there. It was
probably left for me. I hurry and stuff some clothes into
the bag and head outside.

When I get to the front of the house, all of the teenagers are climbing into the back of an open Jeep. It's like a
flatbed truck, but not. It has a cab part up front and in the
back is like a flatbed, but it has seats on both sides and rails
on top of the truck.

I catch sight of Snotty and she gives me this half-smile.
Yeah, yeah. I know. She realizes now she has the upper
hand because she kind of duped me into going on this trip.
Kind of. It was really my decision all along to come.

Ron comes up to me. "I don't want you going," he says. "You're too young and are going through a lot right now."

Realizing everyone is already in the car and just watching us have it out, I freeze. "Are you telling me I can't go?"

"I'm not saying that . . . exactly."

"I want to go."

Avi, who was in the driver's seat, gets out of the car and walks up to Ron. He takes Ron to the side of the house, away from my earshot. I wonder what he's saying. I wonder what they're both saying.

I watch as Ron and Avi shake hands after a few minutes. Then Avi walks up to me. I can tell he's not in a good mood.

"What?" I say.

"Avi assures me he'll look out for you," Ron says, then goes back into the house because *Doda* Yucky is calling him.

"I can take care of myself," I assure Avi when Ron is out of sight.

"Get in the car," Avi orders.

"I don't appreciate being ordered around by you."

"And I don't appreciate a spoiled American bitch delaying my vacation," he says low enough so only I can hear.

If my looks could kill, I'd be staring at a dead guy right about now. Spoiled American bitch my ass. I am *not* spoiled. I know this because I have two parents who want to destroy my life. I mean it. One took me on this trip so he could prove to me he's a great dad. But I bet after the trip he'll go back to his comfy bachelor life. My other parent wants to be rid of me for the summer so she can get engaged to a dork.

If I was spoiled, I'd be surrounded by people who love me. Like Jessica. Her parents spoil her rotten. And I mean rotten with a capital R. She not only has two brothers and a sister, she has two parents who *live* together. They *like* each other, so much so they even hold hands while watching TV. I've even seen them kiss. And this is *after* having four kids. And they're old, like in their forties or something.

To top it off, Jessica's mom makes these little fluffy low-carb cookies that just melt in your mouth. And you know why she makes 'em? I'll tell you why. For the sole reason she knows Jess likes them. Not only do I *not* get fluffy melt-in-your-mouth low-carb cookies, Mom won't even buy anything low-carb at the store. Why? Because my Mom doesn't believe in low-carb diets.

How dare Avi call me spoiled.

Avi walks back around the front of the car and I think he may just drive off without waiting for me. It's like a test.

I hate tests.

What's worse, I feel like this whole trip has been full of tests.

I reach into my pocket and feel the Jewish star *Safta* gave me. She told me the ancient Jewish warrior, Judah Maccabbee, put a six-point star on his war shield. The six points dig into my palm. I'm keeping it in my pocket wherever I go . . . like my very own shield.

When I hear the truck start up again, it doesn't take me long to throw my backpack into the flatbed and jump in.

Within minutes we're on a dirt road, the dust behind us proof of our journey. I have to hold on to the sides of the truck, the rocks in the road make the ride feel like a bumpy roller coaster.

And my boobs are bouncing around like crazy. As if they're not even attached to my body. I thought it was bad enough I had a backpack to be responsible for not flipping out of the truck. Now I have to make sure my boobs stay inside the truck, too.

At least, that's what it feels like. One's bouncing this way, one that way. Every time I cross my arms in front of my chest to keep them in one place, I lose my balance and bump into Doo-Doo (who's on one side of me) or Ofra, (who's on the other).

Can't Avi drive a little slower? It feels like this rocky dirt road has never been traveled before.

The sun is setting over the mountains. It's really pretty to see the reds, oranges, and yellows fade behind the mountains, outlining the landscape before finally disappearing for the night. It's getting darker as we drive, the light fading with each minute that passes. Before long, it's pitch black.

An hour later we finally stop. There's nothing around here, although I can see blinking lights from towns in the distance like twinkling stars in the night.

I forgot since I started this wild journey that I'm in Israel. Otherwise known as the war zone.

Nobody seems to mind as they pile out of the back of the truck. I scan the area as much as I can, which isn't much. I'm still in the truck when Avi comes around to the back of it.

Our eyes meet. "Are you coming out?" he asks.

I still have a bad feeling, as if there's something I'm not getting. And I'm still not over the fact that he called me a spoiled American bitch.

When I don't answer, he shrugs and starts to walk off. I can't see where he's going because it's so dark. But I know he's walking because I can hear the gravel crunch beneath his feet.

"Wait!" I say.

I hear the gravel stop. Then I hear him coming closer to the truck. He's staring at me, I can sense it.

"I, uh, need help getting out of the truck," I say lamely.

I feel his hand shoot out and reach for mine. I grab it and he leads me gently to the edge of the truck. Before I know it, he's released my grip and I feel both of his hands surround my waist as he lifts me from the truck and sets me safely on the ground.

We're both standing there, face to face as he keeps his hands on my waist and doesn't release me. His grasp almost feels like a caress and I don't want him to let me go. I feel safe when he's touching me, even though in the back of my head I can still hear him calling me a spoiled American bitch.

Just thinking of it makes me stiffen and I take a step back.

"Do you mind keeping your hands to yourself?" I find myself saying.

He drops his hands from my body and says, "Be careful for snakes."

"Snakes?"

As if I wasn't stiff enough at that moment. He walks away from me and I hear him give a short laugh. Snakes? Is he kidding?

"Don't worry," Doo-Doo says as he hands me a flashlight. "He's just trying to scare you."

"Well he's doing a good job of it," I mumble under my breath.

I watch as the girls sit down, close to where the guys are trying to start a fire. And I'm standing here by the Jeep.

I should have brought Mutt, he'd protect me from snakes and rude boys. Getting attached to the pup wasn't my idea, he just kind of got under my skin. Even though he is an annoying, Ferragamo-stealing beast.

19

*I hate when others know more
about me than I do.*

"Are you okay, Amy?" Ofra says. She's sitting with everybody next to the fire pit.

"Just super," I say.

I keep my backpack in the back of the Jeep and join the girls. They're talking in Hebrew. I'm used to that by now even though it still annoys me.

I have to sit there and smile when they smile, and like a dork I even let out a laugh when they laugh. I'm like a dumb mimic, because I don't even know what they're talking about!

For all I know they're saying, "Amy's got a booger sticking out of her nose." Then I go ahead and laugh right along with them, which makes it funnier to them but makes me and my hanging booger look like one big loser. When I think of this, every time they laugh I pretend to scratch my nose and feel for anything foreign hanging from my nostrils.

"So, tell me about American boys," Ofra says, and I could just kiss her for starting a conversation with me. "Are they as cute as I see on television? I like the boys on *The Young and the Restless.*"

Believe it or not, I watch *The Young and the Restless.* Maybe I actually have something in common with an Israeli girl after all.

I give them all the scoop on the soaps. I can't believe they're so behind on the episodes here.

"You know so much," Ofra says.

I'm feeling a bit better now, thanks to Ofra. Even Snotty seems to be listening to me without my famous sneer on her face.

After about an hour of laughing and talking and drinking and eating, Ofra and I go off to find a place to pee. But since there are no toilets in the middle of nowhere, we have to squat. Luckily Ofra brought some toilet paper, or else I don't know what I'd do.

We walk away from the group to find a good place for squatting in private. We both have our flashlights on. I'm so afraid of stepping on a snake or other animal I keep the light moving from one side of me to the other.

Now that we're a little ways from the group, should I turn my flashlight off so Ofra doesn't have to see the show of me squatting?

Who cares? I hold the flashlight between my neck and my chin so I can see what I'm doing.

I realize pretty quickly I'm not a good squatter. Especially while trying to hold a flashlight under my chin. In fact, I'm horrible at it. Of course with a toilet I have no problems. Girls biologically weren't made to squat.

As I bend my knees as far as I can without falling, I try to relax. But I can feel the pee dripping right down my leg. So I quickly get into a crab position, with both my hands and feet on the ground. At least this way gravity can aid me in my endeavor.

Dare I look over at Ofra? Can she see me? I should turn off my flashlight, but that's impossible in the position I'm in. And I'm feeling a bit lightheaded. I know what you're thinking. That I'm probably going to fall right into the pee because I'm in a crab position and am feeling kind of off-balance.

But to my surprise, I'm able to keep my crab-pee position just fine. And when I'm done I wipe the best I can and put my shorts back on. I'm utterly proud of myself for this accomplishment. I can probably try out for that show Survivor now that I've peed without a proper toilet.

"Why does O'snot hate me?" I ask Ofra as we walk back to the campsite. I thought I didn't want to know, but I guess when it comes right down to it, I do.

She stops and looks at me thoughtfully. "It's a pride thing."

"Could you be a little more specific?"

"Well, Avi and O'snot have a history . . ."

"I knew it!" I say loudly.

"No, not like that. Well, it's like, uh . . ."

I'm standing patiently waiting for her to finish. Okay, not so patiently. But I don't think she realizes it.

Ofra starts biting a fingernail. "She'd kill me if I told you," she says.

"I'm going to kill you if you *don't* tell me."

"They've always been more than great friends. They've been like brother and sister. Avi used to date a lot of girls, but he hasn't in over a year."

"And . . ."

"Avi's going through a rough time right now. He's kind of been a jerk to everyone. O'snot thought if she and Avi were a couple, he'd get over whatever is eating him on the inside. He rejected her and I guess she's still upset about it."

"She hated me before she even met me."

"Well, she wasn't planning on sharing her room for the summer with an American either."

"What's wrong with being American? I thought the U.S. and Israel were allies."

"We are," she says as we start heading back to the camp-fire. "I guess we get a little pissed off that American kids don't have to join the army while we have to go as soon as we turn eighteen. Girls for two years, boys for three. Don't get me wrong, I want to go. But you American Jews sit in your nice houses on your nice pieces of land and party at your universities while we Jews in Israel put our lives on the line to prevent the destruction of our people and our tiny little piece of land."

"Really? It's that small?"

"The whole state of Israel is like the size of New Jersey."

"No kidding?"

"Nope."

Man, the way it sounds I'm starting to think American kids really do get the better end of the stick.

Ofra and I walk back to the campfire, where the rest of the group is setting out sleeping bags.

Now I panic.

I didn't plan for sleeping bags. Where are the tents? When people go camping back home there's tents. Or cabins. Or teepees.

"I didn't bring a sleeping bag," I say quietly to Ofra.

"That's okay," she says. "I'm sure Avi will share with you."

I blink, as if that would clear my hearing problem.

"Come on, Amy," Ofra says as she pushes my shoulder back. "You know Avi likes you."

Avi? *Likes* me? I don't think so.

"He *hates* me," I say.

I look over at the guy, and he's sitting on his sleeping bag Indian style, a guitar resting on his leg. "He called me a spoiled American bitch," I say to prove my point.

"Maybe he likes spoiled American bitches," she says before walking off to join Snotty, Doo-Doo, and O'dead.

"Right," I mumble back, although I know she can't hear me.

And for the first time since I came to Israel, I'm truly confused to the point where I'm getting this weird feeling inside my stomach every time I look at Avi.

Yes, he's hot as all get out.

Yes, he's about as masculine as a guy could get.

Yes, he's helped me with the snake-guts and herding the sheep.

But he's also arrogant, rude, and totally ignorant.

Could a guy like that actually be attracted to me?

On the other hand, could I actually be attracted to a guy like that?

20

Faking it . . .
It's another way of manipulating
people into doing what we want.

We're all sitting in front of the campfire, which is blazing now thanks to all three of the guys. And we're listening to Avi play his guitar. I have to admit, his voice is very soothing. Of course I don't have the foggiest idea what he's singing about because it's in Hebrew. Who knew the phlegm language could actually sound harmonious when put to music.

He's not looking at me as he's singing. O'dead and Snotty are singing along to the music, all very mellow now due to the mood of the night. Doo-Doo and Ofra are holding hands and are swaying to the sounds of the guitar.

Snotty and O'dead are sitting across from each other. He's staring at her googly-eyed while he's singing. She's oblivious.

When the song is over, I say to Avi, "That's a beautiful song. Did you write it?"

I can still hear the hum of the last note as Avi responds, "Yes."

"What's it about?" I ask.

His expression grows serious. "A guy who loses an important person in his life."

I automatically assume it's a girl and hate the wave of jealousy that comes over me. I don't respond. Silence fills the air. I think he hates me, but somehow I'm getting this weird feeling there's some sort of pain behind his words.

Thinking about what Ofra said, I can't help but wonder how I can figure out his true feelings for me. Not that I care what they are, but listen, an informed girl is a smart girl.

All indications up until now tell me he resents my presence in Israel and he thinks I'm spoiled (which I'm not).

Silence still hangs in the air. It's as if everyone is waiting for something to happen between me and Avi. Love or hate. Peace or war. I won't give them the satisfaction of knowing what I'm feeling. Heck, *I* don't even know what I'm feeling half the time or where my life is headed, thanks to my parents.

I've been trying to put out of my mind the fact that Mom wants to move to the suburbs. The next thing you know she'll be wanting babies with this guy. I may just be a sixteen-year-old kid, but I do know one thing: I am not, I repeat, I am NOT changing dirty diapers.

Just the thought of moving makes my stomach weak. Maybe Jessica's parents will let me move into their condo for junior and senior year. I could even pay them from the money Ron puts in the bank for me. Normally I wouldn't touch that money, but pride hasn't been a word in my vocabulary since coming to Israel. Why should anything be different when I go home?

While I've been daydreaming, I notice the rest of the group has started getting into their sleeping bags.

Only I don't have one. I scan the area. There's three guys and three girls now that Moron has left for his army service. I could sleep with Ofra, but she and Doo-Doo have found a spot off to the side and they've zippered their sleeping bags together. I didn't even know they were a couple until tonight.

Avi is putting his guitar back in its case. There's no way I'm going to ask Snotty if I can sleep with her, she was the person who manipulated me into coming on this little "survivor" vacation in the first place.

Avi knows I'm just standing here watching everyone. This sucks, because I want to make him squirm. Oh, great. Now he's walking up to me. Instead of waiting for him, a light bulb goes off in my brain.

Now I've got a plan. Okay, it's not well thought out and it does require some manipulation, but I think it will have the desired consequence.

I ignore Avi advancing on me and hurriedly crouch next to O'dead.

"O'dead," I say really sweetly. I imagine Avi watching my every move. His eyes are like lasers on the back of my head.

O'dead finally looks in my direction. "Huh?"

Now I'm doing this really big yawn with the arm stretch and everything. It looks authentic, I think. And it definitely gets everyone's attention, except Ofra and Doo-Doo. They're still making out and probably won't be coming up for air for a while.

"I'm really tired and I forgot to bring a sleeping bag," I say, making sure you-know-who hears. "Would you mind if I shared yours?"

O'dead right now looks like a mouse cornered by a cat. By the way, I'm the cat. Meow! O'dead looks from me to Avi.

I'm so tempted to look behind me to see Avi's expression. I'm also wondering what Snotty thinks; she seems to be oblivious to everything else around here.

Before the poor guy can answer me, I say, "Thanks," and go back to the car where there's some privacy to change into my PJs.

I have a huge grin on my face and I don't even know why. I know Avi was going to offer his sleeping bag to me, like he's playing the hero or something. Then he could have more ammunition that I'm a spoiled American bitch who's ruining his vacation. Screw that. I'm going to stay away from him as much as possible on this trip.

Starting with sleeping with O'dead.

Of course I'm not actually going to *sleep* with O'dead. Just sleep with him. Although as I think about how small the sleeping bag is, I'm probably not going to get much sleep tonight.

I can't believe it's getting so cold outside. It's so hot during the day I could fry an egg on a rock in seconds. But now, as I take my bra off underneath my T-shirt and hurriedly change into another shirt, I've got goose bumps all over my body. Brr! I wish I'd thought to bring sweats.

I bind my hair in a high ponytail, brush my teeth with bottled water from the back of the truck, and trot quickly back to O'dead's sleeping bag. I'm rubbing my forearms with my hands to keep warm, but it's no use.

"It's so cold," I say to nobody in particular.

Avi's the only one in his sleeping bag. The rest have gone off to who knows where.

I unzip the bag and examine the interior.

"What are you doing?" Avi asks.

"Checking for snakes," I say before making sure the bag is safe and start zippering it back up. "You know, you should do the same. I wouldn't want you to get bit or anything."

He sits up and regards me with those big, dark eyes. "I bet you'd like it if I got bit."

"No. What I'd like is if you'd leave me alone. You're eighteen. Don't you have to join the army or something?" I say as I settle into O'dead's sleeping bag.

I suddenly realize as I try to lay down I'm *sans* pillow. That means without. Avi throws his at me and it hits me in the face. I grimace, but take the soft thing as Avi turns around and lays down, his head resting on his bent arm. I should feel guilty about taking his pillow, but I don't.

"In two months," he murmurs.

I sit up. "What?"

He doesn't answer. Instead, he says, *"Lyla tov,* Amy."

I don't know much Hebrew, but I've been in Israel long enough to know *lyla tov* means "good night." He's trying to piss me off. I just know it.

I unzip the sleeping bag and stand up. Then I walk over to Avi and crouch next to him. His eyes are closed. Faker.

"Helloooo?"

He opens one eye. "What?"

I sigh loudly. "A second ago, you said two months. What's in two months, besides me leaving this awful place that's as hot as hell in the day, but as frosty as the North Pole now."

He doesn't move, just says with eyes closed as if he's talking in his sleep, "I start basic training for the IDF in September."

"What's the IDF?" I ask.

"Israeli Defense Forces."

Basic training in the Israeli Defense Forces? I feel a little bit bad for Avi he has to go join the army whether he wants to or not.

"I'm sorry," I say.

This time he opens both eyes. "For what? I'm proud to be able to protect my people, my country. What do you do to protect yours?"

What a bitter, bitter dude.

"I do enough," I say. "If Israel didn't piss off all its neighbors then maybe—"

He leans forward, his expression hard. "Don't you dare judge my country. Until you've walked in our shoes," he says, "you have no clue what it's like to be Israeli."

I'm trying not to be nervous, but the way he's talking makes me shake a little.

"Yeah, well, don't judge my country either," I say back.

I start to get up. He grabs my wrist and pulls me back down.

"That's the difference between us. I *am* my country. You're just a product of yours."

Yanking my arm away I say, "That's not the only difference, Avi. I'm going to college and will be successful after high school. And you, you'll probably just be a dumb Israeli sheep farmer the rest of your life."

Stomping back to O'dead's sleeping bag, I feel better thinking about how now I really proved to him I am a bitch.

I undo the sleeping bag once again to check for any fanged creatures who have decided to nest in the place I'm going to sleep. Luckily, there are none so I zip the thing back up and shimmy inside.

Looking back at Avi, I see his back is to me. Good.

Unfortunately, just as I'm getting comfortable O'dead and the gang come back. I'm trying to take up the least amount of space possible, but it's no use. This bag wasn't made for two people.

O'dead kneels down and climbs into the bag with me. I give him a small smile. I don't want him to think I'm not grateful he's agreed to share his warm sleeping bag with me. But I definitely don't want him to think I'm coming on to him either.

He might suspect I'm going to rip his clothes off or something. *As if.* I haven't even done more than kiss my own boyfriend. I'm what you call a sexually slow girl. Because I know what they teach in sex ed is actually true. There *are* real-life consequences to having sex before marriage.

Like AIDS.

Like other sexually transmitted diseases that last a lifetime.

Like an unwanted baby—like *me!*

There's no way in hell I'm going to risk bringing a baby into this world without being married to the man I love. Unlike both of my parents. I mean, what were they thinking? Don't get me wrong, I'm glad to be alive. But the crap I've had to go through my whole life, including this trip and my mom's brain fart by agreeing to marry Marc is ruining my life.

I mean, if we were a normal family I'd be in heaven—not Israel.

Great. Now I'm lying spoon-style with a guy I'm not even remotely interested in. In fact, I know he likes my cousin.

How do I get myself into these situations in the first place? This sleeping bag is way too small for the two of us. And I'm painfully aware my mongo boobs are pressed against O'dead's back.

Closing my eyes, I pray sleep will come fast. But now that I can't see, my other senses are heightened. Like the sound of the fire crackling, the crickets chirping. Like the masculine, musky scent of Avi lingering on his pillow. Like hoping my nipples aren't poking O'dead's back because it's so damn cold outside. It's all keeping me awake, which gives me a great idea.

I wait five minutes before I start snoring.

Of course I'm up, but I have to make it sound authentic. I make sure my mouth is close to O'dead's ear before I start. First, I make this long, slow snoring sound that doesn't really sound like a snore at all, but loud breathing.

Keeping my eyes closed, I breathe in loudly and exhale with the back of my tongue vibrating against the roof of my mouth.

O'dead shifts, probably attempting to wake me up. Only I'm not really sleeping so it doesn't work.

I snore a little louder, and this time add a little nose and extra back-throat noises with just the right touch.

I continue this for a few minutes, ignoring his fidgeting and restless moving around in the sleeping bag made for one-and-a-half. In fact, I should be up for an academy award for this performance. Some would say it's not nice to trick people. But listen, sleep is more important than anything. And if I don't get enough sleep, I'm going to be crabbier than I usually am come morning.

Heavy breath. Exhale loudly. Nose and back-throat combo. Exhale softer. Nose only. Exhale loudly. Heavy breath. Exhale normal.

I'm mixing up the order so it sounds authentic. Genius, right?

The finale is coming. I know it, but nobody else does.

Heavy breath. Exhale softly.

Here it comes . . .

Sleep apnea-type choke as loud as possible. Exhale normal. I know how to do this because Marc snores. Mom thinks I can't tell when he sleeps over because he leaves at five in the morning or something like that. The guy sounds louder than a train wreck. I wonder how Mom can stand it; it keeps *me* up half the night and my room is way down the hall.

I do another one of those obnoxious apnea-type snorts and sure enough O'dead starts wiggling out of the sleeping bag.

Mission accomplished.

I hear O'dead walk away and I squeeze one eye open to spy on him. I know he's going to ask Snotty to sleep in her sleeping bag. Ha! I am so sneaky.

But as my one eyeball scans the area inconspicuously, I get a weird feeling someone's watching me. Then I realize why I feel that way. Avi's looking straight at me, and he gives me this I-know-you're-a-faker look with those depthless, brown eyes of his.

He's getting to be a real pain in my ass.

I give him a harrumph, quickly shut my eye and go back to pretending I'm sleeping.

21

If humans were meant to be in water,
we would have been born with fins.

"Amy, wake up."

I squint to the sound of my cousin's voice and the early morning sun.

"I'm sleeping," I say, then shut my eyes and turn over.

"You can sleep later," Snotty says. "We're leaving in five minutes."

I moan, because as I stated earlier I'm not a morning person. Heck, sometimes I'm not even a day person. I turn back around and squint my eyes open again as I look at her.

"I thought this camping thing was supposed to be a vacation."

"Yeah. So?"

"Yeah, so . . . why wake up before you have to?" I say.

Snotty crouches down and whips the pillow out from under my head. Which, by the way, slams down on the rock beneath it.

"Ouch!" I yell. "Give that back!"

But she's not listening to me because my dear cousin's back is facing me as she walks away. With, I might add, my pillow under her smelly armpit.

Okay, so it's not exactly *my* pillow. But it was last night and it was really fluffy and soft and smelled really comforting. I know that's probably not possible. That's just how it felt to me.

Reluctantly, I get up and head over to the Jeep where the rest of the gang is hanging out.

"It's too early," I say in a moaning, groggy voice.

Nobody answers me, they're all packing up their stuff. And they're all dressed. What is it with these people, getting up and dressed at the crack of dawn?

"Ready to go," Avi says to me.

I open my arms wide, showing him my pajamas. "Do I look ready?"

"Maybe there's miscommunication. I didn't ask you if you were ready to go. I'm saying we're going. Now. It's not always about you, Amy."

I give him my famous sneer. "I do not always think it's about me," I say.

I watch as one of his eyebrows rises up in amused contempt. Then he has the audacity to fetch my backpack and shove it at me.

"I'd advise you to wear a bathing suit," he says.

"Why, where are we going?" I ask.

"Kayaking. Down the Jordan River."

When should I break the news to him I'm not going to kayak down the Jordan River, or any other river for that matter? I don't kayak. I don't canoe. I don't even swim well.

But just to show him I don't think it's all about me, I stalk off to change behind some bushes.

When I come back, everything is packed up and in the flatbed truck. O'dead is driving and next to him in the front is O'snot. Of course Ofra is cuddling up next to Doo-Doo. So that means I have to sit next to Avi.

Great, just what I need first thing in the morning. I park myself next to him and make sure I don't make eye contact. It's starting to get warm outside so I have shorts on and a bikini top.

But as we start moving, I realize my choice in tops is not the best. Damn, I forgot the rocky road we're driving on does not bode well for my boobs.

The bikini top I'm wearing is not a support bra, not even close. And when O'dead starts driving faster, I have no choice but to hold on to the railing. Which means my boobs are bouncing around like buoys on a windy day. Maybe I will have a boob reduction after all, detached pinky parts or not.

I guess Avi realizes I'm uncomfortable because he shifts closer to me and puts his arm around my shoulders. He holds me so strongly I don't have to hold on to anything and my boobs are shmushed so tightly they aren't moving, either.

I should pull away from him. I should slap him for holding me like I'm his. But I feel so . . . stable against him. Nothing's bouncing out of control and that's a good thing. So I stay where I am.

Until, minutes later, we finally turn onto a paved road. I yank myself out of his embrace and push my shoulders back in a dignified manner. Or as dignified as I can while wearing a bikini top.

Luckily, as I look at Ofra and Doo-Doo, they're too involved in gazing into each other's eyes to notice what's going on. Good.

Before long, we've turned into a large parking lot. Everyone gets out of the Jeep and heads to the entrance of the place. Except me.

"Come on," Snotty says as she puts on her backpack.

"I'm not going."

"Why?"

"I'll just wait until you get back."

"You'll be waiting a long time, Amy. Moron is meeting us at the end of the river. We're not coming back here for a couple of days."

My heart starts pounding fast.

"Did you say a couple of *days?*"

"Yeah. Don't be scared. Kayaking is fun."

I give a little huff as I think of white-water rapids and all the different ways I could die in the water.

"I'm not scared. I just . . . well, I don't like water all that much. Maybe there's a phone around here and I can . . ."

She puts her hands on her hips and interrupts me, saying, "You're scared, but you won't admit it. If you're such a baby, I'll ride with you."

I pick up my backpack and jump out of the truck, my feet landing on the gravel parking lot with a loud thud. I put on my sunglasses and look up at her. "You don't know anything."

"I know you think you're tough, but you're really not."

I start walking toward the entrance to the kayak place and say, "And I know O'dead likes you way more than a friend."

She runs to catch up with me. "What did you say?"

"O'dead likes you."

"Only as a friend."

I throw my backpack over my shoulder. "I see the way he looks at you. It's definitely more than friendship."

"Can you find out for sure?" she asks with hope in her voice.

I shrug. "You're Israeli," I say. "Why don't you go straight up to him and ask him? You keep reminding me how Israelis don't bullshit or beat around the bush."

"I . . . I can't."

I huff loudly, mocking her like she mocks me all the time. "Okay, I'll ask him for you." We start walking toward the river together. "By the way, I don't *think* I'm tough," I say. "I *am* tough."

22

Being a good kisser has a direct correlation to how much you like the person you're kissing.

Walking with attitude over to the kayak place is hard while I have a sinking feeling in my stomach I'm not going to get out of this situation alive. But at least Snotty will come in my kayak; I see they're only made for two.

Listen, I know if I sink everyone will be happy, including my cousin. Too bad for her if I go down, she goes with me.

I watch carefully as Doo-Doo and Ofra get into the first kayak. It seems unstable, to say the least. The kayak is not one of those hard plastic-made ones, it's a blow-up rubber one. Whoever the hell thought of a blow-up kayak is one dumb sucker. Don't they know one sharp stick poking it or a hungry piranha and the kayak will pop?

"You okay?" Avi asks. I look at him and he's wearing a blue Nike bathing suit with a white stripe down the sides.

I give him a look. "Of course I'm okay," I say. "What would make you think I'm not okay?"

They're all looking at me like I'm a mashed potato.

"Get in," Snotty says as she tosses our backpacks into the kayak.

My eyes dart back and forth between her and the guy who's launching the inflatable kayaks. He looks like he'll push me in if I don't move faster.

"Do you need a life vest?" the guy asks me.

Yes. "No. But this kayak is running out of air," I say as I point to the floating thing. "I think it has a hole in it."

Kayak-Man has the audacity to actually snicker at me until Avi jerks the life vest out of the guy's hand and says to me, "Get in. I'll help you."

"O'snot's going with me," I counter. Then I look at Avi over the top of my sunglasses. "You're going with O'dead."

I say this then push my sunglasses back up.

Before I realize what he's doing, Avi picks me up and throws me like a bale of hay over his shoulder. Then he jumps right into the kayak. It's wobbly and I'm scared and I'm clawing at him and I'm yelling obscenities.

He sets me down on the bottom of the kayak and pushes off with one of the oars.

"Why did you do that?!" I scream, obviously having a very hard time controlling my fear.

He ignores me and keeps paddling our kayak down the river, letting O'dead and O'snot pass us.

"Put on the jacket. It's gonna get rough," he says after he's been paddling for a few minutes.

I thread my arms through the holes, but I can't click the belt shut.

"My boobs are too big for this thing," I say irritably. "It doesn't fit."

He steers the kayak to the side of the river and holds on to a branch to stop us from moving forward. "Lean toward me," Avi says.

I expect him to make some comment about my cleavage which now, thanks to the life jacket, resembles butt cheeks. But he doesn't. Instead, he leans forward and takes the straps, loosens them to make them longer, and fastens them.

When I realize we're not moving and are still against the bank of the river, I look up. Avi is still close to me, his face inches from mine.

Suddenly I start to feel something in the pit of my stomach. Like I'm going to be sick, but not.

He's watching me intensely and his nearness is making me dizzy. Then he leans closer and closer.

"What are you doing?" I ask.

He touches his fingers lightly to my cheek and all I can think about is the softness of his fingertips on my skin.

"I'm going to kiss you," he explains.

At first, I'm dumbfounded.

"I have a boyfriend," I blurt out softly.

"I know," he says as he rubs my lip gently with his thumb.

"And . . . and you're a jerk most of the time."

His lips are so close I can feel the heat of them.

"Amy?"

"Yeah," I say nervously.

"Stop talking so I can kiss you."

Before I can answer with some smart-ass remark, his lips are on mine. And when I say it's nothing like I've ever felt before, I mean it.

I have to be detailed here so you get the whole picture.

So one hand of his is on my face, cupping it gently as if it was porcelain and could break at the slightest touch. Then he slowly brushes his lips against mine, almost as if he's painting each part of my mouth with his.

It's wonderful. It's intoxicating. And it's totally intense to the point that my mind is reeling out of control. Mitch never kissed me like he would treasure and memorize my lips forever.

When he slowly pulls back and drops his fingers from my cheek, I say, "Why did you do that?"

His mouth twists into a wry smile. "Why did I kiss you or why did I stop kissing you?"

"The first one."

He settles on his seat in the kayak and leans back. I hear the birds chirping in the trees and the wind shaking the leaves. As if they're whispering about what just happened between me and Avi. I wonder what they're saying.

"You needed it," he finally says.

Somewhere in all of this my sunglasses have fallen off and are resting on the bottom of the kayak. I snatch them up and push them back on the bridge of my nose before he can tell what I'm truly feeling.

"Excuse me?" I say. I *needed* to be kissed? What the hell kind of comment is that?

He pushes the kayak away from the bank of the river, picks up an oar, and starts paddling. Then he hands me the other oar. What I really want to do is bang him over the head with the thing. Instead, I yank my oar from his grip and say dumbly, "You kissed me."

He shrugs and paddles some more, the muscles in his arms flexing each time he strokes against the small current. "Just forget about it."

As if I could. That wasn't just some little peck—that was like a slam dunk in the NBA playoffs. And it wasn't even a French kiss, but it was more intimate. I don't know exactly what I was feeling during it. My whole being, my whole spirit, was involved. Not just my lips. I know I'm sounding like a geek, even to myself. And before you think it, it wasn't the four-letter word called love.

"Amy?" he says.

"What?" I think he's going to apologize and tell me our kiss was a soul-searching experience and it's changed his life forever.

"Hold on."

"As in 'wait, I have something to tell you'?" I ask.

"As in 'hold on to the kayak, we're reaching the rapids.'"

23

If you start a fight,
I'll finish it.

If I tell you my life just flashed before my eyes, I'd be telling you the truth. Even Avi's kiss seems like a million years ago as I turn around and see the running waves, the bubbling water, and the white, foamy top to the rapids.

"I don't want to die!" I screech.

"You're not going to die," he says loudly above the sound of the massive rush of water. "Just stay on that side of the kayak so we don't tip over."

"I can't swim," I admit to him.

"You have a life jacket on. Just relax. If we tip you'll be safe."

"I'm scared." And all I want to do is have him hold me so I feel safe. I close my eyes tightly as I hold a deathgrip on the sides of the kayak.

"Don't worry, I'd never let anything happen to you. Just talk to me and it'll be over before you know it."

"What do you want me to talk about?" I say.

Does he want me to tell him where I want to be buried or who I'd like to say my eulogy after we DIE in this river? I think he might not be able to hear me because I know he's working hard by the way the kayak is maneuvering around the rapids.

"Tell me about your mom."

Not the best start to a conversation at this moment. I guess it's better than talking about my burial.

"She's going to marry her boyfriend."

"You don't like the guy?"

"Not really," I say emphatically.

"So move in with your *aba.*"

I open my eyes. "My *aba?*"

"You know . . . Ron. *Aba* is *father* in Hebrew."

"I know that. But I'm for sure *not* moving in with him."

"Doesn't he live in Chicago?"

"Yeah."

"So what's the problem?"

"The problem is that he's not my father. Biologically speaking, maybe. We have a lot to work out between us before he can be considered a real father."

"If you say so," he says matter-of-factly.

I'm suddenly aware we've passed the rapids and are now slowly gliding down the river.

"Don't tell me Moses survived going down this river in a basket as a newborn," I say.

He throws his head back and gives a hardy laugh, the first I've seen or heard from him.

"That would be the Nile River, Amy."

"Yeah, well I'll stick to ·bathtubs. They're much less dangerous."

We ride the rest of the way in silence and I rest my head on the rim of the kayak. I hope some sun rays will give me a golden tan and not burn my skin to a crisp. Believe it or not, I'm trying not to think about that comment Avi said to me after our kiss. But, in fact, I'm obsessing about it.

You needed it. Yeah, that's what he said. Can you believe it?

Maybe *he* needed it. Either way, it's not going to happen again. What would I say to Mitch? Maybe I shouldn't even tell him I kissed another guy. It's not like he's going to find out on his own or anything. And it didn't mean anything; it was just an innocent one-timer.

If food falling on the floor gets a five-second rule, shouldn't an innocent kiss get a one-timer rule? Of course it should, although I guess there is this itsy-bitsy-teensy-weensy part of my brain that's nagging me it wasn't an innocent kiss.

And I'm definitely ignoring the fact that there's this itsy-bitsy-teensy-weensy little part of me that wants to try it again. But not because I *need* it, that's for damn sure.

I sit up. Just as I'm about to ask Avi what he meant by his comment about the kiss, we catch up to the other two kayaks.

"What took you guys so long?" Snotty asks.

I instantaneously blush when everyone focuses on us. My eyes dart from Avi to the rest of the gang guiltily.

A sly smile crosses O'dead's face and he raises his eyebrows a few times.

Instead of admitting we kissed and thinking of ways to divert the attention of the others, I take my paddle (which up until now I haven't used) and whack it on the water to splash Snotty and O'dead.

Direct hit!

My cousin and O'dead are shocked, their clothes are soaked, and I feel triumphant. Ha! That'll teach them to butt into my business.

Snotty and O'dead try paddling closer to us and I frantically paddle away from them. Looking over at my kayak partner, I notice his paddle is not even in the water.

"Help me!" I scream while laughing.

"This is your fight, not mine," he says.

To answer him, I stick my paddle in the water and whack it in his direction. Avi is now dripping with Jordan River water.

I stick my tongue out at him, then say, "Now it is your fight."

Oh, I know what's coming next. I'm not stupid enough to think I'm going to stay dry for long. When Avi's paddle goes into the water and out of the corner of my eye I see

O'dead and Snotty's kayak come closer, I just keep whacking my paddle on the river like a madwoman.

Water from all sides is coming at me. Ofra and Doo-Doo must be joining the chaos. Not that I could actually see anything, because my eyes are shut tight. For all I know I could be whacking water all over myself along with everyone else.

Suddenly, it's quiet except for my paddle hitting the water. So I stop and open my eyes.

Of course when I do, I realize it's the oldest trick in the book. Because as soon as I open my eyes, water splashes on me with a vengeance by everyone else.

"Truce!" I scream, especially when I realize how much water has entered the bottom of our kayak. "We're going to sink!"

The splashing stops and I realize we're all laughing together. And it makes me feel like I'm really part of their little club of friends.

By the time Avi and I reach the landing spot, our kayak is miraculously still floating. And waiting for us is a soldier with a machine gun slung over his shoulder.

At first, I'm startled. Then I realize who the soldier is . . . it's Moron, Avi's friend from the moshav. And the bandana I gave him with the peace sign is wrapped around the butt of his gun.

Wow. My gift did mean something to him.

"Hi, Moron," I say when I get out of the kayak.

He smiles at me. "Hey, Amy."

I wish I could take a picture of him smiling like that in his uniform and gun with a peace sign on it. He looks so . . . nice and harmless, not like someone who would actually shoot that gun at people. I could see the caption now in some national magazine: Moron, Israeli soldier.

The way the media likes to twist things around, the caption would probably get read like this: Moron Israeli soldier. Like he's a complete idiot instead of realizing it's the guy's name.

Moron walks up to me and says, "I'll be your military escort for the rest of your trip."

Military escort? Why do we need a military escort?

"You're kidding, right?"

"No."

I don't want anyone to laugh at me so I don't ask the other questions running through my head. Listen, I'm just starting to feel comfortable with these people and I don't want to make myself an outcast again.

We take a minibus and drive for hours and hours. The landscape of this beautiful land is breathtaking . . . one minute we're driving through grassy mountains resembling the rolling hills in *The Sound of Music* and the next we're in the middle of a large, populated city. If that weren't enough contrast, in another hour we're smack dab in the middle of a desert without a tree or house in sight.

Out the window I see Bedouin Arabs herding their goats in the desert. It's as if I'm looking at hundreds of years in the past through a piece of glass.

A half hour later I see military tanks trekking on the desert floor, shooting.

"What are they doing with those tanks?" I ask nervously.

"Target practice," Avi says.

I hope their aim is accurate.

In less than two months Avi will be a soldier, too, learning to shoot a gun. And he's less than two years older than me.

It's the strangest thing. I'm actually getting used to seeing soldiers all around and guns and tanks daily . . . it boggles my mind how different life is here.

We stop off at a little store to get Cokes (thank the mighty lord) and snacks.

I watch through the store window as Avi goes out to the parking lot alone. I pay for my Kit Kat with the few shekels Snotty gave me and head after him.

"Okay, let's have it out," I say.

He turns to me as if surprised I'm cornering him. "What do you mean?"

"Duh! Why did you say back in the kayak you kissed me because I needed it? If that wasn't the biggest copout, I don't know what is."

"What's a copout?"

I roll my eyes. "You know, taking the easy way out instead of admitting you liked kissing me. Admit it, Avi."

"I told your *aba* I would take care of you on this trip and nothing would happen to you."

"Yeah, well you can throw that promise out the window."

"I'm sorry if I led you on, but it's not going to happen between us."

I'm tired of arguing. Instead, to prove my point I reach out and grab the back of his head and pull him toward me. Instantly, our lips touch and it's like I'm in that kayak with him once again. I close my eyes and wrap both arms around his neck, glad when his arms go around my waist and he pulls me closer. I don't care who's watching, I wouldn't change this for the world.

But suddenly he drops his hands from my waist and pulls away. Then I watch in horror as he swipes his mouth with the back of his hand, as if he wants to erase the kiss off his lips.

"I can't do this, Amy. Don't make it hard for me."

Tears are welling in my eyes and I'm not even trying to stop them or wipe them.

"Don't cry," he says, reaching out to wipe a tear streaming down my cheek. "You're a great girl—"

"Don't say that just to try and make me feel better. In fact, don't say anything to me. I get it, loud and clear."

I start to walk away from him and head to the minibus.

"Amy, let me explain," he says, catching me on my arm.

I stand there, waiting for words I'm not sure I want to hear. I look up at his face and for the first time I see something I've never seen before from him. Sorrow. It is so prevalent it makes me scared.

He squeezes his eyes shut for a second, as if the words coming out of his mouth will cause him pain just by saying them.

"My brother Micha died last year in a bombing."

He looks at me for my reaction, but I'm too stunned to say anything. Instead, I hug Avi tight, wishing I could take some of the pain away from him even though I know in my heart I can't.

"I'm so sorry," I whisper into his chest.

We stay that way for a long time. When he pulls back, I notice his eyes are bloodshot. He covers them with the palms of his hands.

"I hate being emotional," he says.

"I'm probably one of the most emotional people I know," I admit.

He gives me one of his rare smiles, then his expression turns serious.

"I like you, Amy. Probably more than I want to admit, even to myself. But I don't want to get serious with anyone right now. I have a nephew without a father and a sister-in-law who just sits at home grieving her dead husband. I'm going into the army next month. If something happens—"

"If I promise not to grieve for you if you die, will that make you feel better?" I say.

He shakes his head. "It's not funny, Amy. I'm going to be trained as a commando."

"Listen, I'm just talking about a summer fling, not some lifetime love affair." I'm not even thinking about Mitch right now. And I have a feeling Mitch isn't thinking about me, either. Avi and I have a connection I can't ignore.

"You're too emotional not to get involved. You could never have a summer fling. Not the way it's been between us, at least."

"Then what about we end it when this little adventure trip is over. If you want to be a coward for the rest of your life, go ahead. But if you want to have a great time with a kickass girl, you're going to have to face your fears." I want to say *please, please, please*, but I don't. Listen, a girl's got to have a little dignity left if she's rejected by the guy she likes.

"Who's the kickass girl?" he asks, pretending to look around for one.

Playfully I punch him in the stomach.

Nothing more is said about our non-relationship, but he kisses me and says, "You ready for this?"

I wink at him and say playfully, "Absolutely."

When he grabs my hand and leads me toward the rest of the gang, I'm not surprised their eyes are wide with shock. Listen, if I were in their shoes I'd think the world spun on its axis a bit too fast to see me and Avi trying out an actual relationship. Even if it's only a non-committed, short fling.

The only thing nagging me in the back of my head is . . . what are the sleeping arrangements going to be like tonight?

Avi is eighteen, and way more experienced than me.

Will he expect more than I'm willing to give?

24

---

*Doing the wrong thing
sometimes feels so right.*

Moron drives us to a hotel. To be honest, I don't know how he found the place. It's in the middle of the desert with nothing else for miles around, or at least that's what it seems like.

The whole ride to Beersheva, Avi and I were really close, almost as if an invisible wall has been lifted between us. I rest comfortably in his arms and even sleep on his lap during the ride. And you know what? He strokes my hair, as if he treasures it. It feels sooooo good, almost too good because I'm getting these tingling sensations all over my body from just thinking about him kissing me again.

But as we arrive at the hotel and head to the front desk in the lobby, I'm getting a bit nervous. Sleeping next to

O'dead was safe and uneventful. To be fair, we never actually slept together because of my fake snoring.

I look over at Avi. I know I couldn't pass the fake snoring past him; he knows when I'm faking. Besides, I wouldn't even want to be fake with him.

But I'm nervous as to what he expects from me. I don't want to be one of those girls who gets in trouble with a guy and then says, "Yes, I slept in the same bed with him, but I didn't expect it to get out of hand . . ." I'm always thinking, *You shouldn't have slept in the same bed with him in the first place, dummy.*

"What are the sleeping arrangements?" I ask Ofra.

"Who do you want to sleep with?" she asks with a hint of sarcasm in her voice.

Snotty dangles three keys in our faces and says, "The girls are sleeping with the girls and the guys with the guys."

I'm relieved the guys and girls are going to be sleeping in separate rooms. Somehow I have the feeling things could get out of hand with me and Avi. Our relationship is so explosive in other ways I'm sure it will be that way if we're alone together.

We settle ourselves into our rooms, take a short *siesta*, and head to the restaurant in the hotel for dinner in the evening.

After dinner, I make it my business to sit next to O'dead as we all sit in the lobby of the hotel.

"O'dead, will you help me with something?" I ask.

He shrugs. "Sure."

I give O'snot a wink and lead him to my hotel room. It's the one I'm sharing with Ofra and O'snot. When we get in the room I motion to the bed and say, "Sit down."

He shuffles his feet uncomfortably. "Amy, I'm not interested in you like that."

I lean against the wall. "Is there someone you *are* interested in? Like O'snot?"

His mouth goes wide. "How did you know?"

I roll my eyes. "It's obvious. And you need a little kick in the butt to make it happen between the two of you."

A knock on the door interrupts us. When I open it, it's Avi. And he's not looking too happy.

"What's going on here?" Avi asks.

I put my arm around Avi and kiss him on the lips to calm him down. "Are you jealous?"

He just stares into my eyes without saying anything.

"I'm trying to fix up O'dead and O'snot," I explain.

Avi's eyes dart from me to O'dead, whose nod confirms what I just said.

I say to O'dead, "O'snot wants to know how you feel, so go to her and spill your guts." When his eyebrows are furrowed I realize my slang English has confused him. "Go tell her how you feel. Now, before she finds some other guy."

He leaves the room quicker than I've ever seen him move before.

Avi grins.

"What?" I ask.

"You did a very nice thing, Amy. Totally selfless."

I turn away from him. "No I didn't. I was just getting sick and tired of watching him look at her like he'd die if she didn't pay attention to him." God forbid I should be seen as soft.

He comes up behind me and wraps his arms around my waist.

"You want to go for a walk?"

I nod.

He holds my hand as we exit the hotel and aimlessly trek down a gravel path. I get a sweet fluttering feeling in my heart just by being close to Avi.

"Tell me more about your brother."

Avi's pace slows and he takes a deep breath. "I don't talk about him much."

"Why?"

He hesitates before saying, "It hurts. Like deep inside here." He points to his heart. "I know, it's not very cool."

I squeeze his hand. "No, it is cool. I mean, it shows you loved him. But you have to talk about it. If you don't, part of your brother's spirit dies along with him."

He stops and thinks about this for a minute. Then he nods his head slowly. "He loved playing soccer. He was way better than me, but he let me win most of the time to boost my ego."

"Sounds like a cool brother to me. You're lucky."

"Yeah." He shakes his head and sighs. "I wish it was me who died instead."

"Is that why you're Mr. Angry all the time?"

"I don't know," he says. "I guess so."

"You can't change the past, Avi. Believe me, I've tried. But it doesn't work."

"This conversation is deep."

I laugh. "You're right."

"Let's talk about something else. Like how much you like me."

I want to say *I am totally into you*, but instead blurt out, "Ofra says you've dated a lot of girls. Is it true?"

This feeling in my heart scares me and maybe I want to push him away subconsciously. If I hear about his other girlfriends, it will be easier to protect myself because I'll distance myself emotionally from him.

"I've dated," he answers. "But not for a while. I was afraid in the kayak I'd be a bad kisser, it's been so long."

"Your kissing was just fine," I say. More than fine. We start climbing a rocky hill next to the hotel. "I want to know more about you," I say as he helps me reach a large rock that sits high on the hill.

Avi sits down overlooking the dark desert on one side and lights twinkling like diamonds from a town in the distance on the other. It's a very romantic setting and I wonder if Avi's taken other girls here. He guides me down and I sit in front of him, between his outstretched legs.

"What do you want to know?" he asks.

A lot, to be honest. But I say the most common question a girl asks a guy, hating I can't come up with something original or something sounding more mature.

"How many girls have you been with?"

"Been with?" he says from behind me. I feel his warm breath on the back of my head as he leans closer to me. I resist the urge to lean back into him and close my eyes. "Kissed?"

I don't want to think about other things he's done with girls so I say, "Yeah. Kissed."

"Including my mother?"

"No, smart-ass, not your mom. You know what I mean. A real kiss."

"A guy isn't supposed to talk about how many girls he's kissed. I'll tell you what. If you'll tell me, I'll tell you."

I give him a look as if I'll kill him if he doesn't spill the beans. "You first."

"I guess about eight," he finally admits.

"Eight!" I say, flabbergasted.

"Why?" he asks, and I can sense the alarm in his voice. "How many have you kissed? I bet it's a lot more by the way you kissed me in the kayak."

I smile at his compliment but say, "Less than you."

Try two, although the first one probably shouldn't count because that was during a camp overnighter and it happened accidentally in the dark.

You might wonder how I *accidentally* kissed someone. Well, I thought I was kissing this guy I liked during a "lights out mashing session" and it turned out to be the one guy who'd kissed about half the girls in the whole camp. I still remember the taste of soap in my mouth from trying to wash his germs out. You know what they say . . . it's like you've kissed whoever they've kissed. Blech!

Unfortunately when the lights came on during the "lights out mashing session" and I was lip-locked with Guy Wrong, Guy Right saw us and then ended up liking Jessica instead of me.

"Seven?"

"No, not seven, you ho," I say.

"You know what, don't tell me. I don't want you to think about other guys you've kissed. And I'm not what you call a ho. Besides, I just want you to concentrate your thoughts on me . . . on us."

"I thought you hated me."

"I wanted to push you away because I couldn't stop watching you." His voice is hoarse and full of emotion. "Sometimes I can't fall asleep at night. I get hot *tinking* about you," he says, his accent deeper than usual.

"You *tink* about me at night?" I ask and by mistake say tink instead of think. "Why?" *Please don't say my boobs.*

"First of all," he says as he fingers the curls at the end of my hair that have started to frizz in the desert heat, "you're beautiful. But the way you handle yourself in every situation with your own style mesmerizes me. You're animated, you're honest to a fault, you've got this feisty personality I just can't help but watch because I don't know what you're going to say or do next. You're very exciting. And to top it off, you have a big heart even though you don't open it up often."

I twist around to face him. "I've never had anyone describe me like that."

"When you tried to push me off the haystack back at the moshav, it totally shocked me."

"Yeah, except it didn't work. You're like one big mass of muscle."

He laughs. "Don't feed my ego. Now tell me what attracts you to me. Besides my big mass of muscle."

"Ha, ha. But seriously," I say, then take my finger and slowly draw a path from the corner of his eye, past the stubble on his chin and end up at his full lips. "Besides you being a gorgeous male specimen, I like the way you were always there for me when I did freak out. Even though you made it sound like a chore, you've helped me with every challenge I've had here. You let me fall on you when Mutt's friends were about to attack me," I say and kiss him gently on the mouth.

"You helped me herd the sheep," I continue, kissing him again, "and you were my hero by washing off the snake-guts."

Before I can kiss him again and continue telling him all of the incredible things I now see in him that I was blind to before, he crushes his lips to mine.

"Amy," he says against my lips. "I think we're about to get ourselves in trouble. How old are you again?"

"I'll be seventeen soon," I say breathlessly.

He says something in Hebrew I obviously can't understand. "We shouldn't be doing this."

"We're not doing anything except kissing."

"Yeah, but—"

"We can kiss, can't we?" I say as I graze my lips down his neck.

"Yeah," he says in a strained, low voice, "we can kiss."

I don't want him to think about my age right now. I want him to enjoy the time and the kissing. Especially the kissing. I press my open lips to his, because I can't imagine right now not touching my lips to his. He deepens the kiss and I follow, only barely aware we've changed positions and are now lying down side by side.

Okay, I've never in my sixteen (almost seventeen) years felt like this before. It's as if I've crossed the bridge from being a girl to a woman just by experiencing the strange, unfamiliar, steamy sensations deep in my body. My bodily reactions have intensified tenfold as my knight with an Israeli accent caresses my back. I feel like I'll die if we stop and I sense he feels the same.

"I'm going to remember tonight when I'm in basic training," he says as he nips my earlobe. "When they try and wear me out, I'll recall this moment and get through it."

My body feels like it's enduring sweet torture and I want to learn everything about Avi and his body right now. I grab his head to bring it closer to me and then I caress his body with my fingertips. Our lips and mouths are exploring each other's and our hands are doing the same.

When I touch his back, his muscles tense beneath my fingers. My hand moves around to the front of his shirt and I pull the material up to feel his smooth skin and hard six-pack against my hand. His heart is beating fast; I can feel it pumping in an erratic rhythm.

Moving my hand lower, I reach the waistband of his jeans and glide my index finger inside the band. Slowly, my fingers move downward.

Avi groans softly and gently takes my hand and guides it away.

"We can't . . ." he says.

"Why not?" I ask breathlessly, still reeling from our intense kisses. I feel drunk (although I've never been drunk, I can sure guess how it feels) and out of control.

"Besides the fact your *aba* would kill me?"

Great, my dad's not even here and still he's able to ruin my life.

"I don't care about what Ron thinks."

"You may not," he says as he sits up. "But I do. I don't want either of us to regret anything tomorrow."

I sit up, too. "I won't regret anything." Ever.

He kisses me on the top of my forehead. "Let me take you to your room. It's getting late."

25

---

*Approach me
at your own risk.*

"Boker tov," Avi says good morning to me in the breakfast buffet line the next morning. He leans forward to kiss me, but I pull away.

"What's wrong?" he asks.

Duh! He totally rejected me last night.

"Nothing."

I continue to place whatever is in front of me on my plate. I barely realize it's this creamy stuff with whole pieces of little sardiny-like fishes inside (with the silver scales attached, thank you very much). It is DEFINITELY not like sushi. It's gross, but now that I've put it on my plate, I'm going to have to stare at it while I eat.

Before I can add more to my plate, Avi grabs the dish out of my hand and puts it on the nearest table.

I put my hands on my hips. "Hey! That's my breakfast."

I realize I'm making a scene. I don't care.

He grabs my hand and leads me toward the exit. "It'll wait. We need to talk."

He leads me into the lobby and out the front doors. A blast of steamy, hot desert air smacks me in the face.

"Okay, talk. Before I melt, please."

He rubs his eyes in frustration. Next thing you know he'll be running his fingers through his hair.

He looks straight at me and says, "You think last night I stopped things from getting out of hand because I didn't want to be more intimate with you?"

"Bingo," I say sarcastically. "But I'm wiser this morning and won't throw myself on you anymore. Besides, it's not like we were going to have sex or anything."

"Where you and I go physically, our emotions are starting to follow. I can't deal with that."

"You're right. God forbid we should be emotional people. We should just call ourselves 'friends with benefits.' Or, better yet, why don't we just call this whole thing off so you can find another girl to be non-emotional with," I say as I head back inside before my armpits get damp through the shirt I'm wearing. In hindsight, I'm glad I decided to borrow Snotty's tank top.

"You are so stubborn," he says.

I turn around and face him before I reach the door. "I am not."

"Amy, you're the most stubborn person I've ever met. You play games in your mind and create drama that isn't there just to piss everyone off, including yourself."

I just stare incredulously at him.

He takes my hands in his. "Look at me." When I don't he says again, "Look at me."

I raise my eyes and look into his, which are wide and sincere.

"I wanted more last night," he says. "Don't lie to yourself and think I didn't. I beat myself up about a million times after I left you. Believe me, I *want* you to throw yourself at me. But this thing between us is more serious than we're admitting to each other. You're leaving in a couple of weeks whether I want you to or not. And I'm going into the army for three years."

I can't argue his points, so I just stand there staring into his brown eyes.

He lets go of my hands and says, "You want to call it off right now, just say the word."

Then he just stalks back into the hotel and leaves me here in the hot desert heat, sweaty armpits and all.

Damn. Why does Avi have to be so logical about everything? I hate being logical. But I'm too hot to have an attitude and realistically Avi is right. We're getting too attached already.

Slowly I walk back into the hotel and enter the restaurant. Avi is sitting down at a table, talking to his friends. There's an empty seat next to him with my plate on the table in front of it.

I know for a fact I don't want to end it with him right now. I want to keep this thing going for as long as possible.

Our eyes meet and he gives me a short smile. The problem is everyone else is looking at me, too. Okay, I guess I deserve it for causing a scene. I want to cringe in embarrassment, but I hold my head high and sit down next to him.

I avert my eyes from everyone around us, including Avi. But when he reaches for my hand under the table and gives it a squeeze, I squeeze back. *I can handle this relationship* I tell myself. Even with its ups and downs.

"Have you ever been to an alpaca farm?" Ofra asks me.

"What's an alpaca?" I ask.

"It looks kind of like a llama," Avi answers.

"Cool."

Ofra pats me on the back. "We're going right after breakfast so make sure you're ready."

By ten in the morning, we're parked at the entrance to the alpaca farm. Then we pay for bags of food to feed the tall, furry animals with long necks. I expect the alpacas to be in cages, but they're all running around. We actually walk into the large enclosure with them.

I regard the alpacas warily. They're all shades of brown, red, black, and tan. And their bottom teeth are so huge they look like alpaca hillbillies.

I watch avidly as Avi holds out a handful of food for a large speckled gray and black one. It eats it straight from his palm.

"Watch out," I warn. "He could bite your hand off with those massive buck teeth of his."

"They're harmless," he says. "They won't bite you. Try it."

I look at the brown bag of food I've just paid ten sheckels for. Ten sheckels for the risk of getting a huge buck alpaca tooth in your palm. No thank you very much. I walk up to a small baby alpaca and just pet it. Its fur is soft, but a bit wiry. And I laugh when she looks at me with her big gunmetal eyes and large underbite. My orthodontist, Dr. Robbins (otherwise known as Miracle Worker to his patients), could have a field day with this animal.

I feel like I can try and feed this one because it's small. And she looks at my brown bag the way I look when I see a good sushi restaurant. I reach in the bag and pull out some 'feed'. The little bugger can't even wait for me to situate the stuff in my hand before she noses it with her face and scoops it all up with her choppers.

"Hey, don't you have any manners?"

The alpaca starts chewing the food in a very unladylike manner; little pieces of food are falling out of her mouth with each chew.

"Watch out," Ofra says as she walks up behind me.

"For what?" I step back several steps, away from the animal. "Avi . . . Avi told me they're harmless."

"They are," Moron chimes in. "But they spit."

"Whad'ya mean, 'they spit'?" I say, moving farther back away from the buck-toothed spitter.

"Well," Snotty says. "It's more like a loud growling-like burp, then spit. At least they give you warning."

As if having the small alpaca after my brown bag wasn't enough, once they hear me close my bag the noise alerts about ten of the large ones and they come after me, too.

"I'm not an animal person," I say as I run toward Avi. "I'm not an animal person," I chant repeatedly until I reach him.

"They love you," Avi says. "Look, they're all following you."

I place the brown paper bag with the 'feed' (what exactly is inside this stuff to make it 'feed'?) into his hand and hide behind him.

The fearless Avi takes the whole bag and dumps it into one of his palms. As he feeds the things, I hear what Snotty was talking about . . . this loud growl-like burping sound. I crouch farther behind Avi in fear.

"Shit," I hear him say.

"What?" I can't see anything because I'm still behind him.

"It got me."

"Who got you?"

He turns around and I see, stuck in Avi's hair, a slob-ber-phlegm spot with little pieces of chewed-up 'feed' inside it.

"Ew, gross!" I say, stepping away from him.

"I got spit on trying to protect you from it."

"You're my hero, now get away from me. It's totally grossing me out," I say, then laugh at him.

"It wasn't that long ago I washed the snake off your foot. That was pretty nasty. Now give me a kiss," he says, moving toward me.

I hide behind a laughing Ofra. "I did *not* ask you to kiss me after the snake incident."

He stops. And looks so cute all 'feed' encrusted and vulnerable. I walk up to him, keep my distance, and pucker so it's just my lips touching his. Then I pull back. "Now you have to wash your hair." Then I add, "Twice."

26

History is something that should be remembered but never repeated.

Our next stop (after Avi washed his hair in the sink back at the alpaca farm) is a place called Mount Masada. I've never heard of it and I wonder why a "mount" could be a place people would want to go.

But as we drive (And I realize the vast majority of Israel is a barren desert. I truly wonder why it is so sought after.) and we come up to Mount Masada, I ask Avi, "Why are we going to this place?"

"To show you a piece of the history of your people. I think you'll like it."

My people? Who exactly are *my people?* I'm not sure myself, even though the rest of the gang thinks I'm Jewish. The fact is I've been brought up as nothing. Mom doesn't believe in religion, just like she doesn't believe in low-carb diets.

We used to light a Christmas tree for the holidays until I realized at the age of seven Santa wasn't a real guy. They should honestly tell the older kids on the school bus not to tell the first graders the truth about the tooth fairy or Santa. You'd be surprised what kids learn on that yellow bus.

Well, after I found out Santa wasn't real, I told Mom I didn't need a tree anymore. The tree didn't symbolize Christianity or anything. It symbolized Santa. Since the reality of Santa was gone there was no reason for a tree anymore. That was the extent of my religious experience, which wasn't really religious in the first place.

I gaze at the reddish-colored massive thing called Mount Masada as I get out of the car. Everybody is taking their water bottles out of the car and I wonder why they aren't staring at the mountain.

"How old is it?" I ask no one in particular.

Moron, with his ever-present gun strapped to his shoulder, says, "The war here was in seventy-three."

I turn to him. "Nineteen seventy-three?" I guess.

"No. Earlier."

"Fourteen seventy-three?"

"No," Doo-Doo says. "Just plain seventy-three."

Just plain seventy-three? "You mean, like, almost two thousand years ago?"

"Yep."

I gaze again, this time more carefully, at this important mountain in the middle of the Israeli desert. I try to imagine a war here two thousand years ago between the Jews and their enemies.

"I wonder what it's like up there," I say.

"Well, you're about to find out," Avi says as he hands me a water bottle. "You'll need to drink regularly or you'll get dehydrated during the climb."

"You think I can climb this thing?" I ask.

"I know you can, Amy. Like your ancestors before you. See that winding snake path?"

"Do they call it a snake path because it's infested with snakes?" 'Cause I'm tough, but I've had all the snake experiences for one trip, thank you very much.

"It's called that because of its shape," he says, only temporarily reassuring me.

We walk closer to the bottom of the 'mount' and I can make out the narrow, winding path leading to the top. I watch as Doo-Doo, Snotty, Ofra, O'dead, and Moron start their ascent up the mountain. Off to my left I see a big cable coming from the top. I follow where it leads and the end is a cable car situated at the foot of the mountain.

"Why don't we take the cable car?"

Avi starts toward the supposedly non-infested 'snake' path. "Because then you'll miss the great sense of accomplishment of actually reaching the top on your own. I've done it many times and it's like nothing else."

I follow Avi to the start of the snake path. At first it's easy . . . if I just put one foot in front of the other I'll be at the top in no time at all.

But twenty minutes later, I'm panting and my thigh muscles are starting to quiver. I mean, Illinois doesn't have mountains, let alone hills, and I'm not used to it. I slow down, and Avi stays right with me. I know he could go way faster up the mountain.

"Go ahead," I say as we reach about midpoint of the thing. "If I don't die of heat exhaustion, I'm going to die of drowning in my own sweat."

He shakes his head.

"I mean it."

"I'm sure you do. Now get those feet moving so we can reach the top before sundown."

I do it, only because he grabs my hand and guides my limp body.

"Who were the Jews fighting here?" I ask. "The Palestinians?"

"No. The Romans."

Why would the Romans want to come here?

"Then why do the Jews hate all Palestinians?"

He stops and turns to me. "We do not hate all Palestinians."

I snort in disbelief. "I'll believe *that* when I see it on CNN," I tell him.

Finally, the top of Mount Masada is in sight and it's only taken me an hour to walk up the thing. I can't believe I've actually climbed it.

When I reach the top, the ancient ruins amaze me.

"So, the Jews won the battle with the Romans here?" I ask.

O'dead says, "Not really. Jews committed suicide here."

"Huh?" I say, shocked and a little creeped out.

Ofra steps in front of him. "Our ancestors climbed Masada and lived up here during the war. The Romans were at a loss, they couldn't safely climb the mountain without being attacked from the top of Masada."

Avi leads me to one of the ruins. "It is said nine hundred and sixty Jews lived here. They fought as long as they could, but knew it wouldn't be long before the Romans' weapons would be able to reach the top of it. If they were captured by the Romans, they would be killed or sold into slavery."

I look over at Moron, who's gazing down onto a colorful tile mosaic inside one of the homes built inside the mountain. It's absolutely beautiful and it touches my heart people lived on this mountain to save themselves and their families.

"So they committed suicide?" I ask.

Avi continues, "They agreed as Jews they should be servants to God and God alone. To be sold into slavery wasn't an option. They would rather die bravely as free people than become slaves at the hands of the Romans."

"They destroyed all of their possessions except their food supply so the Romans would know it was not starvation that led to their demise, but to show they preferred death over slavery."

My knees go weak from the story and I get chills all over my body. I can't believe how strong-willed the Jews were . . . and still are. I aimlessly walk on the flat-topped mountain and take in all of the half-walls made of stone my ancestors built.

Touching a brick with my fingers, I imagine the women and men two thousand years ago knowing their chances of survival were slim, but having enough courage to build beautiful homes for themselves that would last thousands of years.

As I scan the top of the mountain, I see a group of soldiers reach the top of Masada and congregate together. I notice little pockets on the sides of their army boots.

"What are those little pockets in their boots?" I ask Moron.

"Americans call the identification tags around a soldier's neck 'dog tags'?"

"Yes."

"Well, Israeli combat soldiers wear tags around their necks and one in each shoe. In case their body parts are separated during combat, they can be identified. It is Jewish custom that every person be buried with all body parts, so every effort is taken to make sure that happens for our soldiers."

Wow. What a somber thing to think about.

"What are they doing?" I ask him as I watch the soldiers gather together and recite some Hebrew words.

"They're taking an oath here 'Masada shall not fall again'," Moron explains. "This is a very spiritual place for all Jewish people."

As if the rock I was touching is hot, I pull my hand back. "Ohmygod," I say, and stumble backward.

"What?" Avi says, concerned.

"Nothing." I don't want to admit Masada is a spiritual place for me, too. And for the first time since coming to Israel I know why I'm here and it scares me.

I remember what *Safta* said. *Being Jewish is more in your heart than in your mind. Religion is very personal. It will always be there for you if you want or need it. You can choose to embrace it . . .*

My past might be shady and blurry, but my future is clearer thanks to this horrible, wonderful, shocking trip to a land so different, but so much a part of me nonetheless.

Looking down the mountain and trying to understand how the Jews . . . my ancestors . . . felt with the strong Roman warriors at the bottom, I realize this country has been a war zone since the beginning of time.

Why should the twenty-first century be different than the first?

27

---

*Sometimes our enemies
are our closest friends.*

"Where are you taking me?" I ask Avi.

As the others were eating breakfast our last morning in the south of Israel, he borrowed a car from the rental agency in the hotel and is taking me for a drive. He won't tell me where we're going, though, so I'm nervous.

"To meet a friend."

As we drive over the barren, dirt road, he looks at me with those dark, mysterious eyes.

"You scared?"

"Should I be?" I ask.

"No. You should never be scared with me."

Gee, most of the time I am scared to be with him. But mostly it's because I'm afraid of my own feelings, which are out of control when I'm with him.

I put my hands in my lap and stare out at the beautiful scenery. Who knew rocks and the desert landscape could be so beautiful and so different from the grassy mountains of the moshav.

We're listening to Israeli music on the radio, but I need to get rid of my nervous energy. I start my butt exercises. Tighten. Release. Tighten. Release.

"What are you doing?" Avi asks.

I look over at him and say casually, "Butt exercises."

He stares at me for a second, then bursts out laughing.

"It's not funny," I counter. "If you sit for a long time, your butt'll look like one great big blob of jelly."

"We wouldn't want that, would we?" he says.

I shake my finger at him. "Go ahead and make fun of me. You'll be sorry when you have the biggest butt on the moshav." I lean back in the car seat. "Before you make fun of me you should try it out first."

"You have a nice butt." Avi's lips twitch in amusement. "Okay, tell me how to do it."

"Not if you're going to make fun of me." I don't want to make a fool out of myself again.

"Come on," he urges me. "I won't make fun of you. I promise."

"Fine," I say.

I take a deep breath and realize I'm about to tell a very masculine boy how to do butt exercises. I want to cringe with embarrassment, but he actually looks serious.

I say quickly, "You just tighten your butt muscles like this and then release. The longer you hold the tightened part, the harder it gets."

I attempt to demonstrate the action and feel like a complete dork.

But then I look over at him and he's actually trying the exercise. I can tell by the concentrated look on his face.

"Do you ever vary it, tightening one cheek then the other?" he asks.

I try to suppress a giggle, but I can't. In fact, I can't stop laughing as I watch Avi trying to tighten each cheek in rhythm to the music playing on the radio. He's making fun of himself, emphasizing each movement of his butt along with the rhythm of the song.

I try it, too, and can't stop tightening to the beat of the music. It's contagious, and I'm having one of the best times of my life.

"I didn't know you could be so funny," I tell him, still trying to keep my giggles to a minimum, but having a hard time of it.

"Yeah, well, you caught me off guard."

"Be off guard more often," I say in a very flirty way and smile at him when he looks over at me.

He shakes his head and sighs in resignation. "You're going to get me in trouble with Ron. I told him I'd take care of you."

"You are."

I mean it. Avi was a royal pain in my butt (pardon the pun) when I first got to Israel. But now that he's opened up and let me into his personal life, I feel closer to him than I've felt to anyone in a long time. Even Mitch.

And I realize now Mitch and I are not compatible. In truth, he probably doesn't even know me. I keep a wall of my own up so I don't get hurt. I like Mitch. But I think if he knew me, I mean REALLY knew me, he wouldn't even consider being my boyfriend.

Why? Because I'm high maintenance, for one thing. And second of all I need a strong guy to take my crap and give it right back to me. I guess Avi's a little bit like Ron in that respect. Could it be I'm compatible with a guy who's a mirror image of the Sperm Donor?

We turn onto a small, paved road and drive for another fifteen minutes.

"Where are we?" I ask as he parks the car in front of a small house.

He opens his car door. "Here."

"Where's here?"

He smiles this great big smile, comes around to my side of the car, and opens my door. I know it's considered the gentlemanly thing to do, but let's be honest. I am no lady, and Avi . . . we'll, he's no gentleman. He's a rough, rugged Israeli who can whip bales of hay around effort-lessly. Just the way I like 'em.

I step out of the car and survey my surroundings. I was wrong before—at the moshav it's the North Pole compared to this place in the middle of the desert. I seriously think if I break an egg on the street, it'll be cooked from the hot sun in less than ten seconds.

There are houses in front of me, made of cement, and they're all the same. By that, I mean the houses are all white. No brick, no paint . . . just all white cement.

"Who lives here?" I ask quietly. It's like a little village in the middle of nowhere.

He walks toward the entrance to one of the primitive houses, and I follow dumbly.

"Palestinians," he answers.

WHAT!

Why would an Israeli take me to a Palestinian person's house? I want to ask questions, but I don't have enough time because the front door to the house starts to open.

A teenager, about our age, opens the door. His skin is darker than mine, about the same shade as Avi's. In fact, if Avi hadn't told me this guy was a Palestinian, I would have thought he was Israeli.

I know current events. You'd have to live in a cave not to know Palestinians and Israelis do not see eye to eye on anything. And that's putting it mildly.

But as I watch this Palestinian guy shake Avi's hand and pull him into a short embrace, once again what I know and who I know is tilted on its axis.

"Tarik, this my friend, Amy Barak. She's an American."

Nobody's ever called me Amy Barak before and I'm taken aback. I was born by the name of Amy Nelson because that was my mother's maiden name. Am I Amy Barak?

Some part of me, way deep down, likes the way it sounds. Or maybe I like the way it sounds coming out of Avi's full lips.

Either way, it doesn't matter. I'm nervous. I do everything in my power not to bite my nails or act as shocked as I feel on the inside.

But Tarik smiles, putting me a little at ease. And it's a real smile, not one of those fake ones people do just to be polite (like Marc does). No, this smile of Tarik's reaches his eyes.

"Come in!" Tarik says eagerly. "It's been a long time, friend," he says to Avi as he pats him on the shoulder.

"How's university hunting?" Avi asks him.

Tarik chuckles. "Not worth talking about. Although I did get a letter from UCLA and Northwestern. So tell me, Amy, what brings you here?" he adds as he leads us to a small room.

There are pillows in the middle of the floor and lining one wall. Tarik motions for us to sit. I watch Avi as he sits down on an orange pillow and I follow his lead, sitting down on a light blue one.

"I came with my father for the summer," I say.

I watch as a woman, wearing her head covered and in full traditional Muslim attire, brings a tray of fruit and sets it in front of Tarik. She doesn't say anything, just sets it down and leaves.

Tarik picks up an orange and hands it to me. "From our tree outside. I bet it's better than in America."

I look at Avi, who takes a cluster of grapes off of the tray and starts eating them. Only after I start peeling my orange does Tarik take his own. Is that his custom, to let his guests eat first?

I just can't believe I'm sitting in a Palestinian's house and he's feeding an Israeli Jew and an American stranger. With a smile on his face, no less.

"Are you two dating?" Tarik asks.

"Only for the summer," I chime in as my face gets hot with embarrassment. "That's all."

Tarik laughs. "And after the summer?"

He directs the question to me, but Avi says, "After the summer she goes back to her country. She's got a boyfriend back there."

"Ah, the story gets more interesting now. I think I like these American women."

Avi pops a large, green grape into his mouth. "Please, Tarik, don't let her fool you. Amy *lsanha taweel*."

"Excuse me?" I say. "If you're going to talk about me, speak English so I can defend myself."

Tarik looks at me with a mischievous look on his face. "He says you have a sharp tongue, like a snake."

My mouth opens wide and I say, "I do not. Apologize," I tell Avi.

"Amy, you should know this guy doesn't apologize," Tarik says. "It's not in his nature."

Avi chuckles as he pops another green grape into his mouth, finishing the last one. "Tarik, you should be a lawyer instead of a doctor. You like to argue both sides of an argument, confusing everyone."

Shuffles from the door interrupt us as two girls come into the room with cups and a teapot. They set the cups down in front of us.

"These are my sisters, Madiha and Yara."

Gosh, my life is so different from these girls. They smile and bow slightly in greeting and I stand up and do the same although I feel a little underdressed. I wonder what they think of me. I don't cover my head or wear long robes like they do and I imagine how different our lives are.

After they leave, I sit back down and take a bite of my orange. It is as sweet as if I licked a spoonful of sugar. Yum!

When the sisters leave us alone Avi says to Tarik, "Amy thinks all Israelis hate Palestinians."

The last thing I want to do is start a political discussion with these two and here Avi is, bringing it up. I almost choke on my orange. When I'm finally able to swallow, I open my mouth to say something. Nothing comes out.

Tarik leans back and says, "The Palestinians hold claim to the same land as the Israelis. There's no way around that fact."

"But," Avi continues, "not every Palestinian hates every Israeli and not every Israeli hates every Palestinian."

"How can you guys be friends?" I ask. I turn to Tarik and say, "He's going into the Israeli army!"

Tarik shrugs. "This is his life, what he must do. Mine is not so different. But my people have chosen to fight in a different way; it's the only way my people think is effective."

"Nobody wins," I say. "Why can't you just come to some kind of agreement and stick with it?"

"Hopefully in the future things will change," Tarik admits. "To some, peace with the Israelis is not an option. Me? I want peace, but I also want my people to live their lives respectfully."

Avi looks at me and says, "Many Israelis want the same thing, Amy. Peace, but with the guarantee our women and children can walk in the streets or ride buses without having to worry about their safety."

"But what comes first?" Tarik asks.

"In the Middle East, nothing has ever been simple," Avi says.

"Right," Tarik agrees. "We are both strong people in our beliefs."

I shift uncomfortably on the pillow. "If you saw Avi on the battlefield, would you kill him?"

Tarik looks straight at Avi and says in a bold voice, "Yes. And I would expect no less from him."

Avi leans forward and takes my hand in his. "I brought you here to show you we're not all filled with hatred and here you are asking if two friends would kill each other. Way to make this meeting turn around, sweetheart. Listen, we both do what we have to do to survive. It's our way of life."

We stay at Tarik's house for a little while longer, the guys laughing about school and their families and asking me about my friends back home. They stopped the political discussion; it seems like they know their limits in talking about it. It feels good to discuss stuff without feeling like I have to act a certain way or answer a certain way to fit in.

I like Tarik. And I have newfound respect for Avi because I know he puts aside his political beliefs and befriends Tarik because he's a guy with a good heart and mind. The news makes it look so different from the reality; I think news programs should show the positive sides of people instead of focusing on the negative.

When we're ready to leave, Tarik gives me a hug good-bye and says, "Take care of my friend."

God, I feel like a weight is on my shoulders now. Life in Israel is hard compared to the teenage life in America. Our biggest worries back home are what movie to go see or what outfit we're going to buy. And after high school, we obsess about what college we'll get into. September Eleventh changed our lives, but we still have it easier than the people in the Middle East.

Israelis don't even go to college after high school. They have to put their lives on the line and enter the army. *Take care of my friend*, Tarik just said.

It's not as easy as one might think, especially when that statement comes from a guy who is on the other side.

My own life and the way I've pushed Ron away flashes before my eyes and I feel a little sick. I do have a family here in Israel, maybe I should act like I care about them. If Avi and Tarik can care about each other, maybe I can find

a little piece of my heart to love Ron. And *Safta*. And, dare I even think it, Snotty.

I mean, Osnat.

But what if they disappoint me?

I watch as Avi and Tarik shake hands and slap each other on the back. A smile crosses my face. Because I know, even if they don't, they would protect each other with all of their power even if face to face on the battlefield. Both of these guys have pure, true spirits.

Peace between the Israelis and Palestinians? Who knows? Anything is possible. Maybe, just maybe, the friendship between these two strong-willed guys is a sign of hope for the future.

28

---

*There's a lot to learn by venturing
off the beaten path.*

"How did you meet Tarik?" I ask as we're driving back to
the hotel.

"Let's just say I helped him when he needed a friend,
and he did the same."

"I'm glad you took me to meet him," I say.

"And I'm glad you're here with me," he says, then
adds, "I knew you wouldn't believe me if I told you not all
Israelis hate Palestinians. You're the kind of girl who needs
proof. You shouldn't rely on television so much."

"I don't trust people in general."

"I bet if you did it would open your eyes to a more
colorful world out there."

"Probably. But at least I don't get let down too often because I already expect people are going to disappoint me."

He slows the car and stops it on the side of the road. Then he turns to me. "I want to thank you."

Suddenly my mouth is dry. "For what?"

"For making me remember there's a world out here worth living."

"How did I do that?" I ask.

"You're the first person to make the pain of my brother's death bearable." He kisses me, right here in the car on the side of the barren desert road. "When I'm with you, I'm whole again."

I smile, inside and out. But I'm embarrassed so I look down and finger the heavy silver chain hanging from his wrist.

"You want it?" he asks.

"If you want to give it to me," I say back shyly.

He takes it off and fastens it to my wrist.

"It's like you're telling everyone you're mine," he says. "At least for now."

I lean toward Avi and recapture his lips with mine. Like before, his kisses are drugging me and I'm feeling dreamy and lightheaded.

Before I realize it, I'm lying on top of him. I can feel his hard body under me, the warmth and strength of his muscles beneath mine.

"We should stop," he says.

I nibble on his ear and say, "Uh huh."

He throws his head back and moans. "I mean it, Amy. We're in a rental car on the side of the road."

This time I lick a path from his earlobe to his mouth. "Uh huh."

"You want to wear me down, don't you?"

"Uh huh."

I like the way I make him feel when we're together. I also really like the wild sensations running through my body right now, too, as I move my body against his.

When I feel him start to give in to my hands and mouth, I stop and sit up. I mean, we're in public and any-one could just peek in the window. Would the windows steam up if we continued? I didn't think it could get hotter in the car than outside, but I'm feeling pretty toasty even though the air conditioning is on.

He licks his lips slowly and opens his eyes. "I can't move."

I laugh. "Did I make you forget to be angry all the time?"

"Definitely."

"Good. I can do this forever if it'll make you happy."

His fingers move to my shoulder and he slides the strap on my tank down. "I wish . . ." he says, leaning his head forward and lightly kissing my shoulder.

I know what he wants to say. I want him to say it, but then I remember our little agreement. No getting too involved.

Too bad, I'm already so into him it's scary.

But I know he would regret it if we did go too far. And we are, in fact, parked on the side of a road. "If you don't stop kissing me like that, I'm going to rip all your clothes off," I say.

A little moan escapes from his mouth and he leans back. "I'm crazy about you."

"Good. Remember that when some pretty Israeli girl hits on you after I'm gone. Now let's get back to the others, or I really am going to follow through with my threat."

A half hour later, when we turn onto the road leading to the hotel, Avi says, "So what's the story with your parents?"

He asks me this loaded question and I turn toward the window. "I don't want to talk about it."

"Why not? Lots of parents get divorced."

Yeah, only my parents were never married to begin with. Try telling that story to your peers at school. I always feel they think my mom just slept with a random guy in college and got pregnant. And the sucky part about it is, it's not far from the truth.

"Tell me about *your* parents," I counter. "I never hear much about them from Ron or my aunt and uncle."

"There's not much to tell. My mom works as a teacher on the moshav and my father is your uncle's partner. Okay, your turn."

I take a deep breath. "My parents were never married and I should never have been born. I was, shall we say, a mistake. A very big sixteen-year-old mistake."

There, I said it. My face is hot and my eyes are watery. I'm holding myself together as best I can under the circumstances. I've thought about my life and what a mistake it is about a million times. I've never actually voiced it aloud before.

We arrive at the hotel and Avi parks the car in the parking lot. "I'm not a very religious guy," he says, "but I know there's a very important reason you were born."

"You sound like a rabbi," I say.

"No, I'm just a sheep farmer."

"Avi, you are SO much more than that and you know it," I lean back in the passenger seat and sigh. "I don't want today to end."

He flashes me one of his dazzling smiles. "Me either."

I look into his eyes and he holds my gaze for a long minute. We don't say anything more, there's no words that can say what I want to say to him. Or are there? "Avi—"

"Shh," he whispers, covering my lips with his fingers. "I know."

I reluctantly get out of the car and head for the lobby of the hotel.

The rest of the gang is waiting for us.

When I spot Snotty . . . make that Osnat . . . sitting alone in the corner, I go up to her. "I'm sorry I said you wear short shirts, tight pants, and have a sorry excuse for breasts."

Osnat shakes her head in confusion.

I shift my feet and look at the ground. "I mean, you do wear tight pants . . . and your breasts are smaller than mine. But they're lovely breasts. And I'm sure it's the style in Israel to have tight pants."

Her eyebrows are raised as she says, "Are you trying to apologize to me? If you are, you're doing a lousy job."

I open my arms out wide and say, "Give me a break here, I'm not used to being all gushy and apologetic."

Osnat stands up and says, "I'm sorry I said your breasts sag. Your sagging breasts aren't bad, either." Then she holds her hand out for me to shake it. "Truce?"

Wait just one itty-bitty second.

"You never told me my breasts sag!" I say, ignoring her fake truce.

"Not to your face, I didn't," she admits.

I guess I deserved the insult. And I'll keep to myself I've called her Snotty almost since I met her.

We both start laughing hysterically and everybody else is looking at us like we're mashed potatoes. Two mashed potato cousins.

"Can we go for a walk?" she asks.

"Sure."

We exit the hotel and start walking aimlessly in the parking lot.

I kick a rock down the road as I walk. "I didn't want to come to Israel this summer," I say. "And I didn't want to like anyone here."

She kicks the same rock, continuing its journey down the road. "And I was shocked Ron had a secret daughter. I guess in some way I was jealous of you."

Me? A *secret* daughter? Being thought of as a secret sure beats being thought of as illegitimate. "Believe me, you have nothing to be jealous about. At least you have parents who love each other."

"But Ron has the best job ever. You must be so proud of him."

Okay, so you're probably wondering what Ron does for a living. All I know is he's in the security business.

"It's no big deal," I say. After all, everybody's in the security business these days.

Osnat pulls my shoulder back and stops me from walking. "Are you kidding?" she says. "My mom told me he's been hired as a consultant to the Director of Homeland Security in the U.S."

What? I didn't know that. I guess I never even asked him. I've been too busy being pissed off at him for not being Superdad.

"Yeah, well, he doesn't talk about it much."

"He probably can't because it's classified."

I'm having a hard time thinking of Ron as a super-security consultant hired by the U.S. government. After all, I'm used to thinking of him as the Sperm Donor.

Osnat turns to me and says, "You didn't know what he did until I told you, right?"

"I wouldn't be called a daddy's girl, if that's what you mean," I say. "In fact, I'm not close to anyone in my family. My mom's kind of in her own world and Ron isn't exactly the best father. I don't even have a cousin who likes me. Well, besides your brother, but he can't even speak English. If he did he probably wouldn't like me, either."

"You aren't exactly the funnest person around," Osnat says.

"Are you kidding? I have a lot to offer," I say. "For example, I can show you how to put on makeup so it won't look overdone and won't smear. I'm a whiz when it comes to hairstyles, I can even French braid hair. And I can beat most people I know in tennis. What have you got to offer?" I ask, putting my hands on my hips as I wait for an answer.

"I can ride a horse bareback and I'm really good at dancing. And I'm a great person once you get to know me," she says, absolutely certain she's won me over.

I can imagine riding a horse bareback isn't much different from riding in that Jeep on the rocks, but it does have merit.

"And?"

"And I can tell you Avi has changed since he met you. He smiles now . . . something rare since his brother died. I guess I don't mind you've gotten together since you make him happy."

We hug and I feel lucky to have a cousin who can ride bareback. And to be a friend, too.

29

---

*The threat of taking something
away makes us appreciate it more.*

Two days later, all seven of us are back in the Jeep heading
back to the moshav. I'm anxious to see Ron and tell him I
want a fresh start.

We all enter Osnat's house and it seems like the whole
neighborhood is crowded inside. And they all have their
eyes glued to the television screen. I see my little curlyhead
cousin Matan and *Doda* Yucky. I don't see Ron or Uncle
Chime.

The mood is definitely somber.

"What's going on?" I ask. I can't understand the news-
caster who is obviously covering a very important story.

The house erupts with Hebrew, everyone explaining to Osnat, Ofra, Avi, Doo-Doo, O'dead, and Moron what they're so upset about. Except I don't understand any of it.

"There's been a bombing," Avi explains to me after listening to the others. "In Tel Aviv."

"Where's my dad?" I ask in a panic. "Where's Ron?" I need him now more than ever.

Avi pulls me into an embrace. "Amy, it'll be fine."

Tears fill my eyes and I say again, this time directing the question to *Doda* Yucky, "Where is he?"

I don't get an answer and I feel bile rising to my throat. I pull back from Avi 'cause I want to throw up.

"Your *aba* drove to Tel Aviv with Chime to deliver some meat to some restaurants there," she explains.

"They're fine, right, *Doda* Yucky?" I say, crying fully now and not caring a bit.

Tears are running down her face, too. "I don't know. There's a lot of confusion. After one bombing, people ran to help . . . a second bomber . . ."

"Ohmygod," I say.

I may not know Ron well, but I definitely know if people were hurt, he would be one of the first to run and help. The second bomber . . . I can't think about it.

"We don't know where they are," she says. "The cell phone isn't working."

Going into Osnat's room, I frantically rummage through my backpack. In one of my jean pockets I fish out the Jewish star *Safta* gave me. The diamonds are shining back at me, almost as if telling me I'm a Jew just like the rest of my family. We've survived thousands of years even though we've suffered through most of them, I remind myself.

Walking back into the main room, I put my hands over my face. I don't want anyone looking at me right now. I feel so helpless. How many people were injured or died today? I feel sick just thinking about it. I try to push the image of Ron's body lying in the street out of my mind. But what if he's dead and I wasn't there to help him? I need strength because I think I've lost all of mine. I put my hands down and my gaze rests on Avi.

I need him.

I need him so much I don't know what to do with myself.

"Avi," I say as I run into his chest and hold him tight. "Please don't leave me; I don't think I can handle this without you."

"I'm here," he assures me in a soft voice as he strokes my hair. "And I'm not leaving."

That's right, he lost his brother in a bombing. He must be rehashing the pain of his own loss. We can help each other through this.

Holding out the necklace to him I say, "Will you put this on me?"

We wait the longest hour of my life as Avi and I sit by *Safta* in her room and avoid watching the news report. She tells me about her childhood in Israel and her experience when she first came to what she calls 'the holy land'. She's scared, I can tell. The loss of two sons would devastate her.

When the phone rings, I jump up and run to the kitchen.

Doda Yucky is on the phone, and she looks directly at me as she answers it.

My heart is racing.

"Amy," she says, and I lean against Avi for support as I'm preparing for bad news. "It's your *mudder*."

My *mudder!* I hurry to the phone and clutch it to my ear. "Mom!"

"Hi, sweetheart. I heard on the news there's been a bombing in Israel. I'm just calling to make sure you're okay. Jessica called and she's worried, too."

"I'm . . . I'm okay," I say, barely able to make the words out through my sobs. "But . . . I was traveling and Ron was in Tel Aviv . . . and we haven't heard from him and I'm freaking out. I don't know what to do. We're waiting for a phone call but . . ."

"Oh, no. This is terrible, I never thought—"

"Mom, I got to get off the phone in case he calls."

"Okay, okay," she says in a panic. "I'll hang up. Call me back when you hear something . . . anything. Okay? And you stay put. I need you to come back to me in one piece."

"I will, Mom," I say.

When I hang up, the phone rings again. I hand it to Osnat, who's as anxious and scared as I am.

"Ze aba!" she screams to the crowd after talking to the person on the other end of the line. *"Hakol beseder!"*

Avi picks me up and twirls me around. "They're okay!"

I can't believe it. I go into *Safta's* room and tell her the good news. I learn from *Doda* Yucky that Uncle Chime and Ron had stayed at the bombing site to help the forty-plus wounded.

There's a lot of hugging and rejoicing even though we're all full of sorrow for the poor souls whose lives were lost today in the bombings. It's a strange thing to be happy and sad at the same time. I don't know how Israelis deal with it all the time.

Avi waits at the front entrance to the moshav with me, along with Mutt. The little guy is lying next to me, almost as if he's my protector.

"I can't believe what happened. This has been such a nightmare," I say. "I almost lost my father. Before I really even knew him." It's too scary to think about.

Avi says thoughtfully, "But you get a second chance."

I lean against him. "Yeah, I do. And from now on I'm going to make every second count."

"Me too," he says, and gives me one of his amazing kisses to prove it.

When the gate opens and I see headlights from a car, I stand up. The car stops and my daddy, whose shirt has blood splattered on it, hops out and pulls me into his arms.

"Are you okay?" I'm staring at his stained shirt.

"Don't worry, I'm fine."

"*Aba*," I say to him in Hebrew. "I love you so much."

"Oh, Amy, I love you, too."

I pull back and wipe my tears with the back of my hand. "I'm so sorry I didn't say it before. I know I've been treating you badly. I want you to be a big part of my life now. I want to be Jewish, too. And I want to learn Hebrew. Can you teach me?"

"Slow down, I can't catch up with you. I'm still basking in the '*I love you, Aba*' part." I see his eyes getting red and watery. "I never want you thinking I didn't fight to be with you, sweetheart. I screwed up real bad in so many ways."

He wipes a tear streaming down his face and I'm dumbfounded.

"I was hoping this trip to Israel would change everything. I don't want to lose you to Marc. You're *my* daughter, not his," he says as he embraces me.

He's crying like a baby. So am I.

"I thought I lost you," I say as we walk back to the house, letting Uncle Chime drive back all by himself.

Avi has left us alone, too, giving me and my dad privacy.

"I lost you a long time ago, daughter. I'm glad we've finally found each other."

"Do you think you could find room in your apartment for me?"

"You mean it? I'd love for you to move in with me. For a year. For weekends. Forever. I'll take whatever you want to give."

"If you're not too busy with the Director of Homeland Security, that is."

He chuckles and puts his arm around my shoulder. "I always have room in my house for my number one girl and don't you ever forget it."

"You sure you don't have a girlfriend?" I ask.

"Not anyone important enough to bring home to my daughter."

"I think you need someone . . . to take the edge off of you."

"And who should I thank for taking my daughter's edge away? Or maybe I don't want to know."

"He's been a perfect gentleman."

"Who? Doo-Doo?"

"Can you see me with a guy named after feces?"

"His real name is David."

"Huh?"

"Doo-Doo is a nickname for David."

Stupid nickname if you ask me. "It's Avi."

Ron's face is serious now. "He's eighteen years old, Amy. And he lost his *brudder* . . ."

"I know all that. We've helped each other during our trip and I . . . I love him."

My dad's jaw tightens and the muscle in the side of it starts to twitch.

"It's not like *that*. He respects me and I respect him. Maybe too much."

"I have to get used to having a teenage daughter," he says.

I look at him straight in the eye. "No. You have to get used to me."

30

---

*You don't even know what you
want until it's put in your lap.*

Well, it's the day before I have to leave for Chicago. Avi
and I are going on an double date with Osnat and O'dead.

I glance at my cousin, who looks great now that I've
shown her how to put on makeup so she doesn't look like
a dartboard.

She's watching me pick out clothes to wear. I can tell
by the way she's staring longingly at my Ralph Lauren sun-
dress that she likes it.

"I don't like this dress," I say. "You want it?"

Her eyes light up. "Really?"

"Absolutely. It makes my butt look big," I say, and toss
it to her.

I end up wearing a short, slinky, navy skirt and white top with frilly sleeves. It's the first time I've dressed this nice since I've been in Israel. I hope Avi likes it—all he's seen me in is jeans and shorts.

When I hear Avi's voice in the hallway, my whole body is filled with anticipation and I can't stand it.

Mitch is really going to be pissed when he realizes I've fallen for another guy, but it would be impossible to ignore the excitement I feel when I even think about Avi.

Just as I'm about to walk out the bedroom door, my *aba* walks in the room. He sits on my bed and does a double-take. "You're beautiful," he says. "Like your mother. It scares me."

"Would you rather I was butt-ugly?"

His mouth curves into a twisted smile. "Maybe."

"You want me to cancel my date to make you feel better?" I ask seriously.

He looks up. "No, of course not."

"Good. 'Cause I wasn't going to."

"Amy . . ." he says in a warning tone.

"Get a grip, Dad. I'm not going to do anything you wouldn't do at my age."

He stands up and says, "That's it. You're canceling this date."

Osnat walks out of the room and comes back with her mom. *Doda* Yucky says something to Dad in Hebrew. He sits back down, obviously defeated, and then *Doda* Yucky leads me out to the foyer.

Avi takes one look at me, smiles, and his hand goes to his heart. "Wow."

Great reaction.

Then he takes my hand, squeezes it, and leads me to his car. Osnat and O'dead are already waiting in the back seat.

"Where are we going?" I ask.

"The disco," he answers.

The disco place? I don't really have visions of spending my last night in Israel in a loud, crowded, smoky bar. But I keep my opinions to myself. He's trying, even if my heart is a little deflated at the moment.

When we reach the place, I notice the line is longer than the last time we were here. Great, now I'm going to spend the better part of this evening in a line. What a bummer.

Avi drives up to the front of the club. Osnat and O'dead get out, and I open my car door.

"Where are you going?" Avi asks.

"Uh, to wait in line like the rest of the people who want to go in," I say sarcastically.

"I'm taking you somewhere else."

I furrow my eyebrows. "You said we were going to 'the disco.' I specifically heard you say the word 'disco'."

He says, "We are. But only to drop Osnat and O'dead off."

When Avi winks at me, I settle back in the car and close the door. I really do have butterflies in my stomach, because now I'm alone with him. I've never felt like this about anyone else in my life.

He holds my hand as we drive away from the club and head up a winding dirt road that probably hasn't been traveled in centuries.

He stops the car, turns to me, and shows me a hand-kerchief.

"Is my nose running?" I ask. I mean, is that a hint or what?

"It's to blindfold you, Amy. Close your eyes."

I close them, lean into him and feel him tie the blindfold around my head while he brushes a gentle kiss across my lips. After he helps me out of the car, he leads me somewhere.

This is exciting, he's exciting. I can't wait for all the surprises he's planned for me.

He takes the blindfold off. "Open your eyes."

I blink a few times before I can focus in the dark.

Candles. Lots of them. Two pillows. And between the pillows is an empty plate.

"Sit."

I follow his instructions.

"Okay, wait here." He sounds nervous, which is so cute. Usually he's so calm and cool.

I take in my surroundings. We're in the middle of nowhere, on some barren, deserted land with crickets ser-enading us. I sit down on one of the pillows and wait. Avi comes back with a Styrofoam carton.

He hesitates before opening it. "Are you hungry?"

"For what?"

One of his eyebrows raises. "You tell me. I have food here but if you're hungry for something else—"

"Food's great," I say, interrupting him.

He gives me one of his awesome smiles, sits down next to me, and opens the carton. When I see what's in there, I get so choked up I have to swallow a lump in my throat.

"You bought me sushi! My very favorite food in the whole world. How did you know?"

The sushi rolls are like little, round happy faces smiling at me.

He hands me a set of chopsticks. "Ron told me."

"I've been going through sushi withdrawal these past few months," I explain. "Do you know what quitting cold turkey like that will do to a person?"

He's looking at me like I'm nuts. But I don't care.

"Want some?" I ask, my mouth already full with a spicy tuna roll. I'm moaning in pleasure as I eat the sweet, tangy roll, the sound coming from my throat automatically.

Avi admits he's never eaten sushi, so I coach him. We share the meal, Avi tentatively trying small bites while I'm shoving the stuff very unlady-like into my mouth. I'll have to remember to tell Jessica Israelis make great sushi.

When we finish the meal, Avi stands up. "I have another surprise for you."

"What is it?" I ask, totally excited. So far this evening is absolutely perfect.

"Shoot, I forgot something." He goes off and comes back with a small bouquet of flowers.

Okay, I'm not trying to be bitchy here. But *Safta* got a whole flower shop from my grandfather. And what does Avi expect me to do with flowers when I'm going on a twelve-hour flight tomorrow? I try not to show my disappointment as he places them in front of me, so I smile as sweetly as I can.

"You don't like the flowers?"

"I do," I say.

He takes a red rose out of the bouquet and breaks off part of the stem. Then he kneels next to me and places the rose in my hair. "I wanted to get you something to remember me by, but I didn't know what you'd like."

"So you got me flowers. That's nice."

He chuckles. "The flowers were from my mom. She's old-fashioned. To be honest, she bought them for me to give to you."

This is not the romantic guy I thought he was. "The sushi was great," I say. "But you're losing brownie points fast, buddy."

"Wait here," he says. "I have one last surprise." When he comes back and I see what he's holding, I can't believe it.

Avi is holding Mutt. The puppy has a blue ribbon around his neck. And he's beautiful. "You washed him," I say, tears streaming down my cheeks.

"He's officially yours now," he says, and places Mutt in my lap. "I've arranged for you to take him back to the States."

I can't believe how fluffy and soft he is now that he's clean.

"Arg!"

"Can I really take him home?"

"Yep. He'll probably have to go through a quarantine period, but—"

I smother his words with my lips, because this is the most perfect night of my life.

We spend the rest of the evening talking, making out, fooling around, and playing with Mutt. Right before we pack up the pillows and candles, I know we have to have The Talk.

"So . . . I guess our summer fling is over," I blurt out, fingering his bracelet still on my wrist. I undo the clasp and hold it out to him.

Avi leans forward, resting his elbows on his bent knees. "Keep it. So you won't forget me."

As if. "I'll never forget you. And I realize I am a spoiled American bitch."

"Amy, I'm sorry I ever said that . . ."

"No," I say. "I'm spoiled because I want us to keep in touch and maybe one day, after you finish the army, we could, you know, get together again."

"It's a long way off," he says. "What if you're dating someone?"

"What if *you* are?" I counter.

He laughs.

"You've taught me so much about myself."

He smoothes the stray hair in my face and tucks it behind my ear, his fingertips lingering on my earlobe. When his fingers trail down to the Jewish star still around my neck he says, "You really are a gift from God, Amy."

"No, you are."

When he leans down to kiss me for the last time, I know for a fact somewhere, sometime, someplace, I'll be kissing Avi again.

And next time, it might just be on the top of Mount Masada.

> *The end of one thing is just the*
> *beginning of another.*

I'm back home in Chicago. Yep, Dad and I actually made the long plane ride back.

I was kind of nervous to tell Mitch about Avi, but when Jessica spilled the beans and told me she and Mitch kind of got together after their Ravinia night, I felt a lot better. Of course I made them both sweat it out for a couple of hours. Then I spilled my own beans and told them about Avi.

My Israeli non-boyfriend is in the army now, training to be a kickass commando. He writes when he can, which is about once a week. I realize from his letters O'dead's name is spelled Oded and Moron is actually spelled Moran (thank goodness for them). Doo-Doo still goes by his nickname, but I hope to change that next summer.

Avi never told me he loved me, but he doesn't have to say it. I know he's worried about me worrying about him and he loves me. He has a hard time saying it out loud. I'm okay with that, for now.

My dad and I are going to spend my summer break in Israel next year. This time, I'm planning a two-week-long camping trip throughout the country. I can teach Dad a few things this time, like when to duck when an alpaca starts to make gurgling noises. Avi will be able to take two weeks off then; I can't wait to see him. *Safta* is doing okay—she starts her next set of chemo treatments next month. I'm sending her a care package today.

The wedding between my mom and Marc with a "c" was okay. Marc and I had a talk before the wedding. I told him he could be a friend to me, but I already have a father. He took the news better than I expected. Ron was at the wedding; he was a great dance partner for me.

I've been living at my dad's apartment until Marc and Mom's new house in the 'burbs (which they decided to build from scratch) is ready, which will be months from now. While I'm here, I have a lot of work to do . . . like teaching Ron how to dress to impress a woman. He's not there yet, but he's on his way to becoming a retired bachelor. All I have to do is find the right woman for him. In the meantime, he's teaching me Hebrew and swears to his friends I'm a natural when it comes to herding sheep.

Me and my religion? Well, I'm taking conversion classes with Rabbi Glassman over at Bait Chaverim (which for you non-Hebrew speakers means House of Friends). Mom was shocked when I told her I'm becoming Jewish. I've made her promise to make sure there are no pork or shellfish products in the food she makes for me. Keeping kosher is part of who I am now.

"Arg!"

Yes, that's Mutt. And yes, my dog has a speech impediment. I can't help but love the little bugger. He eats most of Mom's shoes, but knows to leave mine alone. He also thinks he's a lap dog although he's going to be about ninety pounds when he's full grown. We've been through a lot together and he's teaching me to love animals.

My name is Amy Nelson Barak and I went to Israel for my summer vacation. I learned about my family, my heritage, a beautiful land full of rich history, and love. Wouldn't you know, my ruined summer vacation turned out to be the best three months of my life.

About the Author

Simone Elkeles was born and raised in the Chicago area. She has a Bachelor's degree in psychology from the University of Illinois and a Master's degree in industrial relations from Loyola University-Chicago. She was president and CEO of her own manufacturing company before selling it in 1999 to stay home with her children. Simone started writing young adult and historical fiction novels while raising her kids and has earned numerous writing awards for her work. She is the immediate past president of her local RWA chapter, Chicago-North, where she served on the executive board for over three years. She strives to write emotional stories that touch the lives of her readers.

Simone loves to hear from her readers! Contact her through her website at www.simoneelkeles.com.